King of the Cloud Forests

Michael Morpurgo has been a teacher and a farmer as well as a writer of children's books.

He and his wife, Clare, live on a farm in Devon, where for ten years they have run a special scheme called Farms for City Children. Thousands of children have visited them to work as farmers for a week, tending the crops, milking the cows and caring for the other farm animals. These children, and the Devon countryside, have provided the inspiration for many of his books, which he writes in his shed.

Michael Morpurgo writes of *King of the Cloud Forests*:

Why Yetis? I think I became interested because so many sensible people have sighted them. Why bother to make up such stories? The people who live high in the Himalayas believe in them – and think of them as holy creatures to be respected and left alone. So if they exist (and I think they do) how come they have evaded man with his gun, his camera and his greed, for so long? They must be very intelligent – perhaps more intelligent than ourselves.

King of the Cloud Forests was short-listed for the 1988 Carnegie Medal, awarded to an outstanding book for children.

D1534587

Also by Michael Morpurgo

Why the Whales Came
War Horse
Little Foxes
Twist of Gold
The White Horse of Zennor

Michael Morpurgo

King
of the
Cloud Forests

Piper Books

First published 1987 by William Heinemann Ltd
This Piper edition published 1989 by Pan Books Ltd,
Cavaye Place, London SW10 9PG
9 8 7 6 5 4 3 2
Text © Michael Morpurgo 1987
ISBN 0 330 30560 3

Printed and bound in Great Britain by
Richard Clay Ltd, Bungay, Suffolk

For Sebastian, Olivia
and Léa

1

I am called Ashley Anderson, Ashley after my mother's father so I was told, and Anderson after my father of course, whom I remember so well that I only have to close my eyes to have him standing before me. He was an American by birth, from New England, who grew up with one single-minded and determined ambition – to go to China and spread the word of God. Some people run away to sea, or to join the army. My father ran away to become a missionary when he was fifteen. By then he was already an imposing figure, over six feet tall and broad with it, and able to pass himself off as a twenty-year-old to the Missionary Society who were only too anxious to have someone of his youth and enthusiasm. By the time he was nearly twenty he was establishing his own mission outside the town of Ping Ting Chow. With his own hands he built a chapel and hospital compound, and within a few years had become so successful that he had to send for help. There were just too many people flooding into the mission, mostly for treatment and medicine and not for God; but as my father often said, how you bring a man to God is unimportant, just so long as he comes.

It was only a few yards from the hospital to the chapel and all the patients had to come to chapel in the morning if they did not wish to incur my father's anger; and no one ever wanted to do that. He stood fully a foot higher than everyone else and with his thunderous voice and obvious physical strength was not a person to tangle with. He was feared, respected and even worshipped by the congregation to whom he had devoted his life. I never once heard him preach a sermon to them. He always said Jesus had done that better than he ever could. Example was the only way to bring Jesus to the Chinese. That is what he said, but if example did not work he would resort to persuasion of almost any kind. He was not a man to be thwarted. So they came to the Mission in their hundreds and that was why he had to send for another doctor, and that was why my mother came.

I have no face to remember my mother by, but my father spoke of her so often that I feel I know her as well as if I had grown up with her. My father first saw her, so he often told me, at the railway station in Ping Ting Chow when he went to meet her. She had been working as a doctor at the Mission headquarters in Shanghai for some years. She did not come alone, but with a Tibetan, called Zong Sung, soon to be known by all of us as Uncle Sung. My father adored her the moment he first set eyes on her. "Sent from God," were the first words he spoke to her; and she replied: "Stuff and nonsense, Mr Anderson. Now you'd best help Sung with the luggage. Sung is not my servant, he is my medical assistant. There's a lot of it, Mr Anderson. It's very heavy and you're a lot younger than he is – Oh, and by the way, Sung is a Buddhist and he's staying a Buddhist so don't even try to convert him. If you do he's quite liable to convert you – I know, I've tried."

"Perhaps you haven't tried hard enough," said my father.

"She has," said Uncle Sung.

"We'll see," said my father. And that challenge was to make them allies in life from the first meeting. How often I was to witness their long, philosophical debates, understanding little or nothing of what was said, but sensing always their deep mutual respect and affection.

As the years passed Uncle Sung became the cement that held the Mission together. He was the tireless organiser, the foreman, the negotiator, the peacemaker. As the Mission flourished he became more and more indispensable to my father and mother, indeed it was Uncle Sung that brought them together. I suppose you could say I wouldn't ever have been born without Uncle Sung.

With Uncle Sung's help and encouragement my father courted my mother for a full year before she even realised it. All the while the Mission became more and more overstretched. The people poured in as news of the wonderful new lady doctor from Shanghai spread throughout the Province. Uncle

Sung always told me that it was he who suggested that the two of them went out together into the countryside to take medicine to the villages, and so the two of them set off for the hills leaving Uncle Sung to manage the Mission without them for a few days. When they came back she scolded Uncle Sung for deliberately engineering the whole thing, but asked him to give her away at her wedding.

Uncle Sung told me there were nearly a thousand people crowding into the Mission the day they were married. He himself took over my father's old room in the hospital whilst the newly married couple moved into a house built up against the chapel wall. They only had one year of each other before I arrived. It seems I came awkwardly into this world and somewhat later than I should have done. I was my mother's death knell. The birth weakened her and in spite of all that Uncle Sung and my father could do, in spite of constant prayer, she died six months after I was born. My mother was a grave-stone to me as I grew up. I passed her every day on the way from the house to the hospital, for she was buried in the centre of the compound with nothing on her grave but her name, "Charlotte Anderson".

In one sense though my mother never really died at all. She became the spirit of the place, its guardian angel. My father even named the Mission after her, and each year he would climb up and repaint her name in large black letters above the gate of the compound. Uncle Sung took her place as the Mission doctor and ran the hospital just as my mother had done. No problem it seemed was ever too difficult for him to solve, and my father came to rely on him totally.

As I grew up Uncle Sung became a second father to me, indeed I spent more time with him than I ever did with my father, watching him at work with the patients in the hospital and helping out when I could, making beds, rolling bandages and washing floors. It was not that my father was not loving towards me. He was stern with me certainly, and sometimes even distant, but he was loving nonetheless. It was just that he was always on his way to somewhere else and seemed to have little time for me. I remember him mostly striding off through the gates of the town or running up the steps of the hospital. Uncle Sung went everywhere more slowly, at a speed I could manage, and I could see he liked me to be with him. I was always made to feel wanted and useful. What's more, as I grew up he was more my size too and therefore less daunting to me than my father. A ready toothy smile always shone out from his copper brown face, a smile that never failed to radiate calm and warmth. He was never sour or short with me. Only when he was meditating did I feel I could not approach him. This he did often and anywhere, sitting bolt upright, hands on his knees. It was the only time he ever looked serious.

The Mission school was as crowded as the hospital. There was no building. It was held in the open just inside the gate. There I learned to read and write in Chinese – difficult for me since I spoke English to my father and Uncle Sung was doing his best to teach me Tibetan – and my father would come each day just as we were about to finish and tell us a parable that few of us could understand, or a grisly story from the Old Testament that everyone preferred. I remember he told us once of the dry bones that got up and walked about again, and for days after that we were all walking skeletons rattling our arms and legs and chattering our teeth.

Lin was my particular friend. He did not come every day to school for his father was always keeping him at home as a punishment. He should have known better for punishment did Lin no good at all. To the delight of everyone at school he was always wonderfully wicked. One morning before school began he climbed the tree close to where the teacher always stood during lessons and lay hidden on a branch right above her making ludicrous faces at everyone below. He was only discovered when he fell out of the tree and landed at the teacher's feet. He got up, rubbed his sore shoulder and said, "Sorry I'm late". I cannot remember the teacher's name, but I do remember Lin tormented her dreadfully.

Lin was the smallest boy in the class. I was already a head higher than anyone else and two heads higher than him. I took after my father it seemed. When we were alone I would often carry Lin on my back, because it was quicker that way, and anyway he said he could see better. We always used horses to get down to the river though and he rode with superlative ease as if he was attached to the horse's back. Lin loved to fish – he would turn exultant cartwheels whenever he caught one. He tried to teach me but I never had the talent or the patience for it so I was given the job of killing whatever he caught. He was more successful in teaching me how to swim. He taught me how to float. "You just have to believe you can," he told me and after that I found it easy enough to swim, although I never could speed through the water as he did.

I learned more with Lin than I ever did at school. It was Lin who first taught me that things are not always how they seem to be, how they should be or how I had been told they were. It was from him I learned for the first time that there were some Chinese that disliked and even hated missionaries like my father. There were even people in the town who would burn down the Charlotte Anderson Mission, given some encouragement. Lin told me too of the Japanese invasion and how their armies were marching through China from the East. He showed me with his fishing spear how he would treat them if they ever reached Ping Ting Chow.

"But that's killing," I said.

"So?" said Lin.

"You know what my father says," I told him. "Thou shalt not kill, remember?"

"We kill to eat, don't we?" said Lin, suddenly serious. And so we debated hotly until sunset not only whether it was ever right to kill, but also whether or not Jesus Christ could ever be wrong about anything. Lin was the first person in my

7

hearing ever to challenge directly what my father always called "the word of the Lord". I knew he and Uncle Sung talked about these things but this was different. I worried more about that than the advancing Japanese army. I began for the first time in my life to find it difficult to say my prayers at night and mean them. I had begun to doubt.

Uncle Sung was reassuring about the Japanese. "Do not worry yourself over the Japanese, Ashley. Between us and them is the whole Chinese army. They will not let them pass." I dared not mention what Lin had said about Jesus for I knew he would refer me to my father about such matters. I kept my doubts to myself.

But it was not long after this that we heard for the first time the dull rumble of distant bombing and soon the town began to fill with tired soldiers. The first wounded arrived at the hospital and I found my father and Uncle Sung working day and night alongside a Chinese army doctor who demanded that the soldiers always had to be looked after before the civilians. One evening I remember he insisted once too often. I witnessed my father's anger from the bottom of the hospital steps as he turned on the Army doctor. "Major, this place is for the healing of the sick and that we will do whether or not they are soldiers. We are all God's children in or out of uniform, whatever the uniform." The army doctor looked hard at my father, his eyes blazing with anger. I was quite sure at that moment that my father would be taken away and shot, and I've always thought if Uncle Sung had not intervened that could indeed have happened. Uncle Sung led the army doctor away and pacified him somehow. I don't know what he said, but whatever it was it worked. After that although Father and the army doctor were never the best of friends, they at least tolerated each other.

There was no school any more now and Lin and I sketched out elaborate plans in the river mud for the defeat of the Japanese. They were coming from the south and the north now, Lin told me, and we knew from the soldiers' stories where the battle fronts were. "Let them come," he said fiercely. He was ready for them.

Then one day Lin did not come to the Mission and I was on my own. I rode down to the river bank, but he wasn't there. As evening fell I searched the narrow streets of the town for news of him, but no one seemed to know where he had gone. It was almost dark as I walked back up the hill towards the Mission gates. A small figure came out from the shadows to meet me. He was wearing a uniform. He saluted and laughed. It was Lin. "But you're only fourteen," I protested.

He held up his rifle in front of me. "I can shoot this and that's all that matters," he said. "And anyway I'm not fourteen, not really. I only said that to be the same age as you – I'm not so small if I'm fourteen, am I? I'm sixteen and I won't be much taller by the time I'm twenty. Make a smaller target, don't I?" We laughed and shared a cigarette before shaking hands solemnly. I watched him walk away and vanish into the smoky dark of the town.

The bombers came the next morning, throbbing and roaring above us. Father and I were in the middle of breakfast and we heard the cheering outside in the compound. I remember Father looking out of the window and saying, "What are they cheering about? Can't they see they're Japanese?" Then he was shouting to them to take cover. He pushed me under the table and threw himself on top of me as the first bomb fell.

2

I was conscious of dust and smoke and of Father's weight on top of me. I could hear screaming from the compound and I thought I should say a prayer if I was going to die, but as the fifth and sixth bombs fell, and fell further and further away, I thought there was no need. The drone of the bombers faded and all about me was a terrible stillness.

"Is it over?" I whispered. "Have they gone away? Father? Father, can you hear me? Will they come back?" There was no answer. I twisted under my Father's weight to look at him. His eyes were closed and there was blood in his black hair and on his forehead. I looked past him and only then understood that the house had collapsed on top of us. The table top was on my Father's back and all around us lay the splintered, torn timbers that had been our walls and ceilings. The teapot with the blue fish on it that Uncle Sung had given us one Christmas long ago lay so close that I could reach out and touch it with my fingers. It was broken in half so that the fish

11

was cut in two. There was tea trickling out of the spout, warm on my hand.

I do not think it was the bombing itself that frightened me so much. Indeed I remember feeling momentarily exhilarated that I had survived. It was the growing fear that my father was dead that fetched up the terror from inside me. With my free hand I shook his shoulder and screamed at him to wake up, but he did not. His eyes remained obstinately closed and his body limp and heavy around me. Exhausted at last by my own fear I lay still. Only then did I feel Father breathing rhythmically on top of me. In my confused state of mind it took me some time to understand that if he was breathing then he must at least be alive. I tried again to shake him awake and was rewarded at long last with a murmur and a half smile.

That was how Uncle Sung and the others found us some minutes later. Through a forest of timbers I saw Uncle Sung's sandalled feet, the sun on his dusty toes. He was standing where the chapel wall should have been. There was the sound of whimpering and wailing from the compound beyond and then they were pulling away the timbers to get to us. But they were taking so long, and Father's weight was making it difficult for me to breathe. Uncle Sung was constantly there, encouraging me, reassuring me, and I heard the strident voice of the Chinese army doctor as he organised the rescue. I remember how Lin and I used to imitate his strutting gait and squeaky voice. I'd never really liked the man ever since his argument with Father on the hospital steps. We had put him down as an arrogant, unfeeling man who cared for little except his own dignity. Now here he was urging his men on to yet greater efforts as bit by bit they pulled away the timber and fought their way through to us. Lin and I had been a bit unfair on him I decided.

The rescue was painfully slow – each timber it seemed had to be extracted carefully for fear of further collapse – but at last the table top was being lifted and there were hands grasping at Father's shoulders and pulling him off me. Uncle Sung asked me whether I was all right. I tried to speak but could find no voice. I felt suddenly free of Father's body and saw Uncle Sung's smiling face above me. "Playing hide-and-seek?" he said. "Bit old for that aren't you?" A searing, sudden pain invaded my chest. Uncle Sung's face swam into a dark void full of distant echoes and I slipped away from him. If this is dying I thought, then it's not so bad, just a pity that's all.

I woke to find myself in the hospital. I could feel there was a bandage tight around my chest and my arm was held in a sling. There were three figures at the bottom of my bed who came into focus as they spoke. "At least he was the only one," said the Chinese army doctor. "We were lucky," he went on. "The only bomb that fell in the town itself did not explode. They think nothing of bombing towns. Life is cheap to them. It was more to frighten us than anything else. The nearest Japanese soldiers are a hundred miles away, maybe more. Headquarters have assured me they are no closer."

"But they'll be back, won't they?" said Father. "And you have no planes to stop them with, have you?" There was a white bandage across his head and he was leaning heavily on a stick. "If they can do it once, they can do it again. What's to stop them? You tell me that. And next time we might not be so lucky – it might not be just one boy. One bomb in that warren of a town and there'd be hundreds dead."

"I have faith in our soldiers," said the Chinese army doctor, stiffening. "The Japanese will come no closer, Mr Anderson, I can assure you."

"I have faith only in God, Major," said Father. "Fifty yards the other way and every one in the compound, everyone in the hospital would have been killed. The chapel we can rebuild – we will rebuild; but the first thing we must do after the funeral is over is to paint a red cross on the roof. There'll be some safety in that surely."

"I doubt it," said the army doctor. "The Japanese are barbarians, but you can try."

"Mr Anderson," said Uncle Sung, who had his back to me. He spoke softly, almost secretly. "What do we say to Ashley? How do we tell him about Lin?"

"Let's wait till he's better," said my father, "though God knows where I'll find the courage from to tell him even then."

"I can't think what made him do it," said the army

doctor. "Everyone hid when the planes came, everyone except that boy. He was warned. They told him to keep down. They told him it was no use shooting at planes, but he wouldn't listen. He ran out into the open and began firing. You might as well spit at a tiger. Someone said he was only fourteen years old, just a boy."

I wished at that moment that I had died in the ruins of the house. I closed my eyes and swallowed the scream inside me.

"He was sixteen," I said as they walked away. "He told everyone he was fourteen because he was so small." The three of them turned and stared at me and then my father came back and sat on the bed beside me. "Fourteen or sixteen, he was still too young, Ashley. But we must thank God he was the only one killed. It could have been much worse."

"Not for Lin," I said. "And why did God pick on Lin, Father? What did Lin ever do to God to make him that angry?" There was pain and bewilderment in Father's eyes and I regretted at once the venom in my question.

"I don't know what Lin did, Ashley," he said, the tears coming into his eyes, "any more than I know why your mother was taken away from us so young. I don't know all the answers, but I do know they are together now, Lin and your mother. They are both with God. There'll be no pain for either of them, no more sorrow, and that is why we must be happy for them."

But no matter how I reasoned it during those long days lying on my back in the hospital, I could not be happy for Lin, for mother or for me. Lin was gone. My best friend had been taken from me. I was bitter at a God I no longer loved nor cared to understand.

It was essential, the Chinese army doctor said, that I kept still for I had broken two ribs and there was a serious risk of infection from the gash in my right arm. So I sat in the shade of the hospital veranda whilst my father directed the rebuilding of the chapel and the house. Uncle Sung and the Chinese army doctor ran the hospital together that spring whilst Father turned carpenter, builder and painter. He painted red crosses on the roof of every building in the Mission compound, just in case the Japanese planes came back.

As the weeks passed though I could sense in Father a growing feeling of unease. In spite of the army doctor's continuing reassurances that all was well in the east and that the Japanese were being held in the south, there was increasing evidence to the contrary. The new timber for the chapel did not come through on the train. There had been no post from the Mission headquarters in Shanghai for nearly two months and the vital medical supplies Uncle Sung had asked for never arrived. The post arrived, but weeks late. More and more wounded soldiers poured in through the gates of the Mission and all the news they brought was bad. The Japanese advances had not been halted and the Chinese were retreating on all fronts. Even the government had been forced to leave Peking and move west. As well as this there was the terrible news of the burning of a mission not more than fifty miles away. Two French nuns had been killed in the blaze so the story went. No one was sure whether it was the mob that turned on the mission or a band of brigands. Thinking back I think it was probably this atrocity rather than the Japanese threat that finally persuaded my Father to send me away.

It all happened so quickly and without any warning. It was in the middle of the night that Uncle Sung came to fetch me from the hospital and walked me across the moonlit compound into the chapel that was still waiting for its new roof. Father was pacing up and down, his hands clasped behind his back. He stopped when he saw me and sat me down beside him on a bench.

He began to talk without even looking at me, hands clenched on his lap and leaning forward. "Ashley, I know your Mother would want me to do this, I know she would. I am doing it for her and I'm doing it for you. This Mission is no place any more for a child. We must let Lin's sacrifice be a lesson to us. You've heard what happened to the French Mission, the nuns?" I nodded. "And even if the Japanese do not overrun all of China, as they well may, we have seen already what their planes can do. I cannot leave. My work is here, Ashley, with the Mission. God brought me here and God needs me here. I cannot desert these people. I have the chapel to complete and the hospital will be needed more than ever now. So I shall stay and perhaps I shall follow on later, if God wills it. But you will leave now, you and Uncle Sung." I tried to interrupt, but he turned on me, almost in anger. "Do not make this more difficult for me than it is already, Ashley. I have asked God's guidance in this and I know it is right. Can't you see that if I did what I wanted to do I would go tonight with you and Uncle Sung? It is a lesson to learn in life that we cannot always do what we want."

"Tonight?" I said.

He nodded. "You're fit enough now if you keep your arm clean and the ribs have healed nicely enough. Uncle Sung has agreed to go with you, to take you to India. It's taken weeks to persuade him to leave the Mission but he knows there's no other way, and he knows it's what your mother would have wanted. You'll have to go, Ashley." And my father turned away. I knew from the tone of his voice that he would brook no argument, but I tried nonetheless. "Why can't we just hide somewhere?" I asked.

My father's voice was gentler now. "There is nowhere left to hide. China is in ferment. The Japanese have brought destruction into the very heart of China. Bands of brigands roam the country-side at will and terrorise the people. Missionaries have been stoned to death – yes, it's true, Ashley. Warring factions fight each other everywhere for

18

power. No one is safe in China today, least of all the missionaries or sons of missionaries. For many reasons, Ashley, which you are too young to understand, we are not much loved here." He put an arm around me. "It's all arranged. For safety's sake you will travel as Uncle Sung's son – he has made Tibetan clothes for you. So until we meet again, Ashley, Uncle Sung will be your father. I could wish you no better guardian and guide. He will take you to the mountains in the far west, through Tibet and the Himalayas. It is Uncle Sung's country, he knows it well. And perhaps in the spring of next year you can cross into Nepal and then down into India. As you know, your dear mother was from England and it is the English who rule in India. You will be safe there. I have written to the Mission Headquarters in Delhi. They will I'm sure provide you both with passage to England. And I have written to your grandmother in England telling her to expect you. She will look after you and I will join you as soon as I can."

"But when will that be, Father?"

"When God wills it," my father said quietly and he stood up in front of me. "I shall help pack the horses now. You must be gone before dawn. I want no one to see you leave."

The last I saw of my father was a tall black figure standing in his cassock at the gates of the Mission, waving his stick in the air. He called out, "God bless", and then he was gone, closing the gates behind him. I felt then that I would never see him

19

again. Uncle Sung reached across to me and took my hand. "You're not alone," he said.

The moon skulked behind a cloud and we rode away together, my horse coughing in the cold night air.

3

An hour or so after we left the Mission – it was still not quite morning – Uncle Sung turned off the road into the trees and dismounted. He drew out of his saddlebag a pair of felt boots and a bulky quilted coat with deep pockets just like the one he always wore. "I made it myself," he said with some pride, holding it up against me. The coat was far too big for me and I told him so. "Time will take care of that," he said. "This will be a long, long journey. By the end of it you may well find these clothes too small, but then by the time we reach India you will have no need for them any more." He buttoned it up to my neck. "From now on I am not your Uncle Sung and you are not Ashley Anderson. You are Zong Ho, only son of Zong Sung. We are pilgrims on our way to Tibet, to Lhasa."

Holding my arms out, I could barely see my finger-tips emerging from the sleeves. Uncle Sung laughed, sat me down and set to work on my face. "And you must be dark, nut brown like I am, like all Tibetans are," he said.

Within an hour my hair was blackened with Chinese ink, and a pigtail made of yak hair was plaited into my own hair. The makeup he used to darken my face was a mixture of crushed charcoal and cocoa, and bitter to lick. Uncle Sung worked fast, stepping back and turning my face into the light to consider it more carefully. Lastly, my hands were dusted with charcoal and a round, flat felt cap pushed down on my head. He lifted my chin, stood me up and turned me round. He was pleased with his work. "Zong Ho," he said. "You are now really my son. Two things you must not do. You must not wash, unless we are alone and it is safe; and you must not talk unless we are alone, and then only when I say you can. My son, Zong Ho, was born dumb. He has never uttered a word in his life, not a word."

Not to wash was, I thought, a wonderful notion, but not to talk – that was quite a different matter. I protested strongly. It was impossible I said. I was bound to blurt something out. He took me by the shoulders. Uncle Sung had not often been stern with me, but now he was in deadly earnest. "In China, you are a white man, a foreigner – that is bad enough in these times, but if they discover you are the son of a missionary there are men who would murder you without even thinking about it, men on this road, and me too if I'm caught with you. And in Tibet where I come from and where we are going there are men who believe all 'phillings' are devils, and no one there minds killing devils."

"Phillings?" I said.

"Foreigners. Tibetans call them 'phillings'. You must understand that all men of your race are not like your mother and father. Many of them come only to take what they can and leave. Such people are not welcome, not in China and not in Tibet." He made me walk away from him and turn round and walk back. "Now remember you must speak only when I say you can, when it is safe. You'll do, Ho Zong," he said, "just as long as you don't wash, you'll do. We must go on now. I want to be a long way from here before dark."

We rode out of the trees together into the frail light of dawn. "Goodbye Ashley Anderson," I said, "I'm Zong Ho. Zong Ho. Zong Ho." I liked the sound of the name and said it again and again until Uncle Sung stopped me.

"You may be Zong Ho," said Uncle Sung, "but you're not the son of Zong Sung."

"Why not?" I asked.

"Because Zong Ho, the son of Zong Sung, is dumb," he said. "He has been since birth, remember?"

I thought he would be smiling when I looked across at him, but he was not. As our eyes met I think I understood the seriousness of our situation for the first time. "You must never forget it, Ho. Never," he said.

I was used to riding, but I had never travelled far on horseback before, only to the town and along the river banks with Lin. By that first evening, after a day in the saddle, I was sore and stiff. As I dismounted, my leg must have touched the horse's rump for he started forward suddenly and I was thrown off.

I fell on my side, my arm trapped underneath me. It was not a hard fall; but my chest pained me a bit as Uncle Sung helped me to my feet. My coat was torn. When he took it off to make sure I had not damaged myself I noticed that my arm was bleeding again. The old wound was open. Uncle Sung bound it up and we both thought no more about it. It did not trouble me much. It was a clean wound after all, and almost healed.

I remember well enough the heat and the flies and the dust as we rode across the plains that summer, the filthy water we had to drink, and the rats. I shall never forget the rats, nor the infernal dogs that leapt out at us at every farmstead we passed and threatened to tear us to pieces. Without Uncle Sung's long staff to protect us I feel sure they would have done so. But at least no one appeared to doubt we were father and son. My disguise, renewed each morning, clearly worked. Our story seemed to be believed wherever we went. We were accepted as pilgrims and much compassion was expressed at my unfortunate disability. I began to feel comfortable in my new persona and confident enough to revel in the deception. But my arm was beginning to pain me now and I found it difficult to sleep at nights.

From time to time though I felt I was regarded with some curiosity – not least I thought because I was two or three inches taller than my father (something I could not disguise) – and indeed on one occasion we did come very close to discovery.

For the most part we kept away from others, but sometimes meetings on the road with traders or pilgrims or herders forced us into company. It was the hospitality of the farmers who took us in at night that proved the most dangerous, and it was on just such an occasion that I forgot myself once over supper. The soup on this particular evening was thick with barley and steaming hot and I was famished. I ate ravenously and made the mistake of licking my fingers when I had finished. The eyes of the little girl standing at my elbow should have warned me. I saw the inquisitiveness in her face turn to a look of alarm, and only then realised that my fingers were licked quite white. Uncle Sung had noticed and kicked me hard under the table. Either the girl was too young to speak or too terrified because she ran across the room and buried herself in her mother's skirts, sobbing hysterically. I sat on my hand until I had collected my thoughts and prayed that the little girl would not find her tongue. She kept looking back at me from over her shoulder and then she began to babble incoherently to her mother. Uncle Sung kicked me again and I looked across at him. He was reaching down and rubbing his hand on the sole of his boot, feigning a fit of coughing as he did so. By the time the little girl dragged her mother over to look at me my hand was grimy with the dirt from my boot and quite as dark as the other. She took one look at it, screamed and ran out of the door, her bewildered mother in hot pursuit. I never licked my fingers again.

As we travelled westwards Uncle Sung taught me to understand Tibetan well enough not to look stupid if I was spoken to. I remembered a little of what he had taught me when I was younger, but now I think I was quicker to learn. To speak it though would have betrayed me at once. I was happy enough to be dumb. He taught me how to blow my nose with my fingers as all Tibetans do, and to spit like a Tibetan herdsman, long and loud and often, to click my tongue as he did to show amazement – a practice I did not find difficult for I had in the past often mimicked Uncle Sung's own peculiar way of expressing himself. It did not matter yet, he said, but once we were amongst Tibetans I would need to be more convincing if I was to be accepted as one of them.

We had to walk a lot now as we left the plains behind us that autumn and began to climb higher into the hills. The horses were sturdy, thickset creatures but hardly bigger than donkeys, and with our packs we were a heavy load. To rest them we dismounted at the foot of every hill and walked up. I remember that I found it difficult to keep up with Uncle Sung on the hills and that my arm still would not heal properly despite all Uncle Sung's efforts. It ached continuously now and throbbed down to my finger-tips. I knew I was getting weaker but did not want to admit it either to myself or to Uncle Sung. It was not courage, just obstinacy.

It have a clear picture in my mind of Uncle Sung walking ahead of me, one arm on the neck of his horse and leaning on his staff. Beyond him the sun came up over the mountains and set the peaks on fire. They were the first high mountains I had ever seen. "Tibet?" I called out. "Not yet," said Uncle Sung. "But soon. Soon now." And suddenly my legs gave way and I found myself on my hands and knees incapable of moving. Uncle Sung was helping me to my feet, but I was too feeble even to stand. There was not enough strength in my arms to hold on to him. I looked up. Uncle Sung's face glowed copper gold and flames from the mountains licked about his head.

That is all I can honestly say that I remember of the first stage of our journey. For the missing months of winter I must rely on Uncle Sung's account of my illness and the trek up through the mountain passes of Tibet onto the plateau. The horses were sold and he bought a yak and a cart to carry me and the baggage – a horse cannot negotiate snowdrifts as well as a yak. I have only incoherent flashes of recollection, the stifling smell of smoke, greasy sheepskins, the rocking of a cart and the swaying vision of white mountains against a grey pall of sky, and a cold whining wind biting at my face. I remember, or rather I think I remember because my grip on reality was so tenuous I may well have dreamed it, but I recall lying at night with the stars so close I could almost reach out and touch them; and then there were the strong colours of the high plateau with its dark, deep skies and everywhere rocks of red and yellow.

It seems it was the poison in my arm that nearly killed me. Unnoticed it had affected my whole body. For nearly two months, Uncle Sung told me, I hovered near to death. He found refuge for us in a disused butcher's house in a mountain village, built entirely of bones and horns. The people of the village were used to pilgrims and treated us with great kindness. The house was dry and warm. The yak dung for the fire was brought to the house every day by the villagers, who prayed as Uncle Sung did for my recovery. More than once, Uncle Sung told me, my feverish ravings had almost given us away. Many was the time he had to clap his hand over my mouth in case someone passing by outside the house should hear me. English or Chinese – I raved in both and both were equally dangerous. After all I was supposed to be dumb. Somehow I survived. Uncle Sung never believed in miracles, but he often said afterwards that he now understood why many people did. Reason tells me that if it wasn't a miracle that saved me, it must have been Uncle Sung.

The next spring, when he thought I was strong enough to travel again and when the snows had cleared from the high passes, Uncle Sung decided to move on. So, buried under a pile of sheepskins, each one a parting gift from the villagers, I lay in the back of the cart whilst Uncle Sung led me up into the foothills of the Himalayas.

We followed a well-trodden path now and almost

every day we would meet parties of pilgrims on the road. Uncle Sung tried to avoid them, but it was inevitable that we should often camp with them at night, sometimes in the open but more often we were offered the hospitality of a farmer and slept in his house. The fog of my memory clears now I suppose, because all the while I was regaining my strength and health. I must have been fully recovered by the time I met the lama for I remember clearly every word he said to me. It was a meeting that was to change the course of my life.

That evening we were amongst a dozen or so fellow pilgrims gathered together in an isolated farmhouse. We were relieved to have found it for outside the weather was worsening. We were talking and eating together in a first floor room – like all Tibetan houses, the ground floor was the stables. I was looking out of the window and up towards the mountains, trying to ignore the inquisitive eyes of the farmer's children, when the lama came in through the door. He was dressed in a humble travelling robe tied around the middle with a red belt, and he wore a tall, red cap on his head. The children were silenced for a few moments and settled down to stare at him. Some meat and freshly dug turnips were cut up unwashed and thrown into the pot. When he had finished eating, each of the pilgrims asked him for an omen, or 'mo' as they call it in Tibetan. I knew enough of the Tibetan language now to make some sense of what was being said – Uncle Sung had seen to that. The lama answered each pilgrim patiently in low, considered tones and then turned to Uncle Sung. "You do not ask for 'mo'," he said. "Do you fear for what lies ahead?"

"No," said Uncle Sung. "I have no desire to know what will happen to me on this earth, and what happens to me afterwards I shall deserve – that's all I know. We decide for ourselves. It is in our hands, is it not?" The lama nodded and smiled.

"And your companion?" said the lama.

"He is my son, Zong Ho," said Uncle Sung.

"Bring him where I can see him."

Uncle Sung nudged me to my feet. Reluctantly I got up and stood in the circle of pilgrims, looking down at the lama. He looked me in the eye for long and dangerous moments. I could not hold his gaze. I looked down to Uncle Sung and he smiled encouragement. I was confident enough in my disguise, indeed so confident by now that I had even forgotten that I was at risk, but this man was not looking at my clothes nor at my skin. His eyes reached into my soul and found me out. I felt like running, but the way to the door was blocked by the farmer's family who had crowded into the room. There was no escape.

"He does not speak," said Uncle Sung. "Since the day he was born he has never spoken a word."

The lama's eyes never left my face. And then he spoke very slowly and with great deliberation. "You have a fine son but he has the blue eyes of a 'philling'," he said. The word sent a shiver of suspicion around the room. The lama held up his hand. I think Uncle Sung and I then acted better than

we ever dreamed we could. I feigned furious out-
rage, and blew my nose with my fingers and Uncle
Sung cursed all phillings roundly for good measure.

"My son's eyes," he finished angrily, "are an
accident of birth as is his dumbness. Would you
blame him for that?"

"I did not mean any offence," said the lama. "But
he has strangely light eyes for one of our country. He
is taller than you, taller than any grown man in this
room – and he has the giant feet of a yeti. But it is not
his great size that troubles me. There is something
about him that tells me he is not like one of us. I see a
ruler standing before me. I tell you, this boy of yours
will be a king, and soon." The lama had his eyes
closed now and was speaking in a whisper. "He will
be a king of the cloud forests. He will rule among the
clouds." He opened his eyes. "That is all I can tell.
Ask me no more."

4

I sensed now a brooding hostility towards us. Our fellow travellers scrutinised me intensely, suspicion written on every face. It was our great good fortune that the farmer's children chose that moment to chase each other around the room like puppies after leaves, so drawing attention away from us. It took some time for the farmer's family to settle down in their corner to sleep, and even then there was much giggling and squabbling over the shared blanket. To silence the children, the farmer and his wife had to lie down beside them; and at last they were still, a great bundle of bodies under the blanket. Once they had subsided the others soon followed the lama's example and stretched themselves out on the floor. Soon the room resonated with the sound of deep breathing and rhythmic snoring.

Uncle Sung lay beside me that night as awake as I was. I longed to whisper to him to ask whether I had correctly understood the lama's 'mo' and if so what it might mean. I felt too a strong desire to get up and run, for I was sure that I had been discovered. I had no doubt whatsoever the farmer believed me to be a 'philling' and perhaps many of the others did too. Uncle Sung's eyes glinted in the dark beside me. His finger came up to his lips and he shook his head slowly. So I lay beside him, my mind a morass of hopes and fears and wonderings, and waited for the morning.

But Uncle Sung did not wait till then. I was only half awake, lulled towards sleep by the breathing around me, when I felt his hand pressing on mine. With infinite care we got up and picked our way through the sleeping pilgrims towards the door. It was dark outside; the moon hidden behind the peaks lit the hillside only dimly. Outside the stables we stopped to tie our belts and garters and to pick up our loads. I went to untether the yak that had brought us up the mountain, but Uncle Sung took me by the hand and led me away. The wind was bitter cold. Within minutes I could hardly feel the staff in my hand and my feet were blocks in my boots. We stumbled down the hillside, across the cane bridge that looked and felt perilously near to collapse and followed the trail up through the trees towards the snow line. Once we could no longer see the farmstead Uncle Sung let me rest. I sank to the ground and lay back on my load.

"They knew, didn't they?" I said when I had the breath to speak.

Uncle Sung nodded. "The lama knew and perhaps the others too. We could not risk staying till daylight. I'm afraid they may well come after us now."

"What will they do to us?"

"Nothing, because they won't catch us," said Uncle Sung.

"But if they did?" I asked.

"No one will catch us." Uncle Sung reiterated firmly. "I know these mountains. I was brought up here. They will not catch us, not if we can put an hour or two between them and us. We have a start on them and we must not waste a minute of it. I haven't brought you all this way to be caught now. We'll travel higher than they suppose. We'll go through the high passes. The higher we go the less chance we have of being followed. I promised your father to get you home safely and I intend to keep that promise."

"What did he mean, Uncle Sung? What did the lama mean? He said I'd be a king, a king of the cloud forests. He said . . ."

Uncle Sung laughed as he helped me to my feet. "There's good lamas and bad lamas," he said. "Just like Christian missionaries – there's some you believe and some you don't. I do not know this lama. He may have been talking in riddles to confuse – that way they can never be wrong. They do that sometimes. But he seemed a wise enough man to me. Perhaps it was just his way of speaking. Perhaps he guessed we were going up into the mountains, into the clouds. Who knows?"

"And what's a yeti?" I asked. "He said I had feet like a yeti."

"It is true you do have large feet," said Uncle Sung. "But even so this was a lama with a taste for exaggeration. I myself have never seen a yeti, but they stand, it is said, twice, perhaps three times as high as any man and therefore would have the feet of giants."

"Are they real?"

"Very few people have ever seen them, so few that many say they do not exist at all. But I am sure they do. I had a friend when I was young who saw one with his own eyes – he was a good man and no storyteller. It is said they live higher than any living creature and that they are timid in spite of their size and power. Perhaps that's why so few are seen. They are covered in dark red hair – that is well known – and they can run like the wind, faster than any leopard. There are some people who believe they are gods. But gods or not they are quite harmless to man – no one has ever been attacked by a yeti."

"So you've never seen one yourself?" I asked. "So you can't be sure they're real, can you?"

"I only believe what I know," said Uncle Sung. "I once saw a yeti skin hanging on a wall in a monastery. It was too big to be a bear. No, they are real enough." He looked down at my feet and smiled. "He was right. You do have the feet of a yeti. You'll need them too, where we're going."

He pointed up towards the snow clouds that were rolling over the mountains, clinging to the peaks as they came. "That way lie the Himalayas and the border, perhaps only ten days away now. It's the short way and it's the hard way but it's the safe way. Are you ready?"

It was not snow but hail we encountered later that morning, stinging, driving hail that drove us often into the shelter of rocks. The snow came soon afterwards and Uncle Sung was pleased for he said that no one would set out to follow us in such weather. Clinging to each other for support we climbed into the mountains.

Nights were spent huddled in stone hermitages built into the mountain sides, or if we were lucky in monasteries and villages where Uncle Sung would buy all the food he could, molasses cake, bacon, dried meat, rancid yak butter, tea and 'tsampa'.* We eked out the cake and meat and lived for the most part on hot butter tea and tsampa, a poor enough diet, but sufficient to keep us going.

Each mountain pass was higher and colder than the one before. Our lips were cracking and the chilblains on our fingers and toes were becoming unbearable. My feet began to lose all feeling, even when I warmed them by the fire.

Uncle Sung seemed never to tire, keeping always a steady pace in front of me, stopping from time to time to wait for me. Each day I found myself falling further and further behind. I think I must have split my boot running to catch him up, but if I had, I had not felt it. It was evening before I discovered my left foot was blistered and raw. Uncle Sung stitched the boot together as soon as it was discovered, but by then the damage to my foot had been done. He blamed himself for not having taken more care, and

* 'tsampa' – the flour of roasted barley.

he used the last of the bacon fat to rub into our boots to keep out the water.

More than once we lost our way blinded by the dark or the snow and had to spend an entire day backtracking to find our trail again. I began to lose heart. Food was running short and Uncle Sung had no money to buy any more. We had to beg, and we did. Uncle Sung's cheerful optimism kept my spirits alive during the long arduous marches and through the terrible cold of the nights when we would cling together for warmth. It wasn't that he talked much, Uncle Sung never did that. He was rather my silent support, the strength I relied on to see me through every new day. He rarely spoke of his religion but to watch him meditate each day as he did was to see a man renewing himself. Age did not seem to weary him.

I came to know and love him better than any person I have ever known. Until then he had always been my old Uncle Sung. I think I had always taken him for granted. He had been a fixture, reliable, endlessly protective and loving towards me as I grew up, but now as we suffered together Uncle Sung became my friend and I his. It was a bond forged in adversity, one that would never be broken.

The morning the blizzard came was serene in its stillness. It came with the wind from nowhere. We saw it coming but there was nowhere to hide. We were caught on the open mountainside. There was nothing to do but dig ourselves in, to find shelter in the snow itself. We cowered there under Uncle

Sung's blanket for hours, feeling the snow pile up on top of us, but when the weight of it threatened to collapse and smother us, we had to climb out and go on. To stay would have meant dying of cold. The snow whirled about us and blinded us instantly if we opened our eyes. I hung on to Uncle Sung's belt and followed him. The snow had drifted across the trail behind us and so there was no way down around the mountain. We had to go on, on and up. Neither of us spoke as we struggled on, each of us fighting our own pain and exhaustion.

We knew the next village was down in the valley on the other side of the mountain, two days' walk away Uncle Sung had told me. We knew well enough that to spend the night out on the mountain would finish us. Our only real chance now lay in finding one of the 'dopkas' '* summer camps, the only shelter we were likely to find this high; but as the sky darkened around us and night began to fall even that last hope began to fade. Only the white of the snow lit the bleak world around us now as we limped on. And then I stumbled against a post, a post that became a fence. I called out to Uncle Sung and we followed the fence through the deep snow until we saw solid and square in the darkness ahead of us the outline of several huts. We searched the huts and found firewood in one of them and dried yak dung in others. We occupied the biggest of the huts, the one with the fireplace, and Uncle Sung lit the fire that

* 'dopkas' – herdsmen who graze their stock, usually yak or cattle, in high and inhospitable regions of Tibet.

saved our lives. We crouched over it and soaked in the warmth as it infused our frozen bodies. We ate the few remaining crumbs of our molasses cake – the last of our food – and drank bowlfuls of hot water. We hadn't the energy to speak but fell asleep on the floor with the crackling fire beside us roaring up the chimney.

But warmth and water were all the yak herders' hut afforded us. The wind screamed around the hut day and night, beating against the windows and the door like some enraged beast. We cowered inside, curled up against each other and I prayed it would pass. As the snow piled up against the window day after day hunger began to weaken us, and even Uncle Sung now began to despair. He would not say as much but I could see it in his clouding eyes and his forced smile. We were used by now to doing without food, but before at least there had always been the prospect of food in the next village or the next monastery and that had spurred us on. To try to reach the shelter of the valley in such weather would have been certain death. It was all we could do to dig our way through the snow to the nearest shed to collect dung and wood for our fire. Slowly the possibility of dying in this place became a probability in my mind. I was beyond caring, beyond praying.

Then one morning we woke up to a wonderful quiet and blue skies. The wind had dropped to a whisper. Within minutes we were ready to leave. Flushed with sudden hope and somehow no longer even hungry we laughed together as we fixed each other's loads. I was just tying the last strap on Uncle Sung's bundle when I saw the face in the window behind him. It was a dog's face, at first just one of them, a frosty grey muzzle, and then a second, bigger than the first and dull gold. Their mouths were open and panting. They stared back at me out of cold, cruel eyes. Uncle Sung turned. "Wolves," he cried, and he ran towards the window shouting and waving his staff like a madman. The faces vanished at once from the window.

I knew about wolves of course – what child does not? – but I had never before seen one. At the time I remember not being able to understand Uncle Sung's fear, for they seemed to me to be mere dogs and we had fought off those often enough during our journey. Uncle Sung stood for a moment looking out of the window. When he came back he was trembling. I had never before seen Uncle Sung frightened of anything. "There must be ten of them outside there just waiting," he said.

"Waiting for what?" I asked.

"For us," Uncle Sung said, shaking his head. "You can't blame them. They're hungry just as we are. They know we're in here. They can smell us and they'll wait. And that's what we'll have to do." He shrugged off his load. "Perhaps they'll lose patience," he said.

"But that means we can't get to the barn," I said. "How are we going to keep the fire going? We've only got enough for a day or so at the most."

"I know," said Uncle Sung. "We must be still. We must move around as little as possible. We have to make them forget we're here. It's all we can do."

All day we heard them prowling around the hut. Often they would attack the door, scratching and scrabbling on it so violently that we feared that the hinges might give. The door buckled but held. We did not move except to put more wood on the fire. A gnawing hunger cramped my stomach so that I had to bite my knuckles to prevent myself from crying out. At night, as if to let us know they were still there, they set up a hideous howling outside the door and it was to that terrible lullaby that I fell asleep. When I awoke Uncle Sung was by the window, his load on his back. "Have they gone?" I said, sitting up.

"I've been watching since dawn," Uncle Sung said. "There's been no sign of them. Maybe they went after easier prey, or maybe something frightened them off. Who knows?" He pulled his hat down around his ears. "Ashley," he said – it was the first time he'd used that name since we left China – "I'm going down the mountain to fetch some food. I would rather be torn to pieces by wolves than die slowly of hunger and cold. I still have some strength and I shall make the best use of it." I was on my feet tying my coat around me, but he stopped me. "No, with your bad foot you would only slow me down. You will stay here. I shall be back by noon tomorrow with enough food to build up our strength for the last climb. We are no more than three days now from the highest pass and the border."

I begged him not to leave me though I knew in my heart he was right. I could not have walked a mile in my enfeebled state. Uncle Sung was adamant. "I want you to build up the fire so that this place is like an oven when I get back tomorrow. It's only a few yards between here and the barn. There's plenty of yak dung in there. You'll be safe enough. Whilst the weather's fine fetch in all you can from the sheds around, but make sure you look carefully before you go out, understand? You'll be all right if you're careful. I'll be back before you know it."

I watched Uncle Sung stumble away through the deep drifts, leaning heavily on his staff. The last I saw of him he was turning and waving back at me, knee-deep in snow, and then I was alone with only his footprints outside to remind me I was not the only person alive in this white wilderness.

I set about the task he had left me with a will and banked up the fire with all the fuel that was left in the hut – and that was not much. I boiled some water and sat by the fire, filling myself with warmth. In spite of this my legs below my knees remained numb. My legs and feet were there because I could see them but I had long since ceased to feel them. I went to the window and scanned the snow around the hut again and again for any sign of the wolves. There wasn't a footprint or a scat anywhere – it was all virgin white and unblemished except for Uncle Sung's tracks. I decided it was safe to go out. I was too weak to hurry. I trudged back and forth to the sheds until the back of our hut was piled high with dung and wood.

It was early afternoon by now and I was on my way back with an armful of lightings just in case the fire ever went out and we had to start it again. I was thinking how pleased Uncle Sung would be with me when he saw what I had done, and then I saw the prints, a second track running almost parallel with Uncle Sung's. He was back, back already. In my eagerness I stumbled in the snow and dropped the sticks around me. I never bothered to pick them up. They could wait. There would be food inside. I threw open the door. The creature was crouched by the fire and when he rose his bulk filled the room. He was like a giant man but yet not a man, for he was covered in a coat of long, red hair.

5

I could neither run nor scream. Even when the huge creature lumbered towards me I remained rooted to the spot. Because my head was swimming I raised my hand to steady myself against the door. As I did so the creature stopped instantly, mouth open, breathing hard. He was close to me now, towering above me. Only then did my thoughts gather themselves and it came to me that this might be the yeti creature Uncle Sung had described to me. He was gigantic and was covered in red hair from head to toe. Only the centre of the face was hairless. The skin was wrinkled and black. His nose was flat and turned up so that the nostrils were scarcely more than two holes in his face, and the chin receded almost formless into his neck. His forehead was vast and prominent and overhung the face in a permanent frown. But under the thick red eyebrows the eyes that looked back down at me were searching and intelligent. They were wide with fear or anger – I could not tell which.

Keeping an arm's length away he circled around

me towards the open door. He stood for a moment examining me, his head slightly on one side before turning and ducking under the door. It took me some time to come to my senses. I slammed the door shut after him and ran to the window. The yeti, and I was now quite sure that that was what he was, was bounding away through the snow on all fours. Beyond the barn he stopped, and turned and stood up again. For just a moment he looked at me, and then he was gone and I was alone again. Curiously enough after such a terrifying encounter I can remember that I was sad to see him go. There was no sense of relief that danger was passed, just a feeling that I had somehow wasted an opportunity. Worst of all was the knowledge that I was alone again in this desolate place with only my hunger for company. I felt oppressed by the new emptiness around me.

How much I longed now for Uncle Sung to return and for the food I knew he would bring with him. But as time passed I began to believe that Uncle Sung might not ever come back and that I would be left to die here on my own. The wind got up again whipping the world outside into a raging blizzard. The hut shook so violently that I thought the roof would lift off at any moment. I knew that Uncle Sung could not travel in such weather. No man could.

I piled the fire high again and drank more hot water, not because I was thirsty, more to banish the desperate loneliness and fear that welled inside me. Certainly the crackle and heat of the fire was some comfort. But sleep was the only real way to forget and I slept in snatches all through that day and into the night. I spent my waking hours keeping a futile watch at the window for any sign of Uncle Sung's return. The end of the blizzard brought a welcome silence but no hope. There was no movement outside. The fresh snow had covered all footprints and tracks. It was as if neither Uncle Sung nor the yeti had ever been here.

Once in the half light of dawn I fancied I saw a shadowy figure stalking through the snow in the distance. It might have been a wolf, a bear or perhaps a yeti. Whatever it was I welcomed it, for it was some sign that I was not the only thing left alive in this white wasteland. I was quite beyond being frightened of anything by now.

The next day was the longest I ever knew. I busied myself trying to drive some feeling into my ankles and feet, stamping up and down the hut, but that tired me quickly, and my feet stayed frozen despite all my efforts. To pass the time I began to build a lifesize effigy of my yeti in the ash that was piled in front of the fire. I tried it again and again until I felt it was a fair representation of the creature I had seen. By the time I had finished the ash yeti was stretched out like a giant grey gingerbread man right across the room in front of the fire. I found two black stones for his eyes, a stick for his mouth, and it was done. And still Uncle Sung did not come. I waited by the window all afternoon and watched the sun slip behind the mountain peaks and the shadow of night creep across the snow towards me. He did not come and he did not come. He would never come.

That night I curled up in front of the fire and tried to rock myself to sleep. I was sure by now that Uncle Sung had either been taken by the wolves or that he had lost his way in the mountains or been caught out in the blizzard and had perished with the cold. I knew for certain that Uncle Sung was dead and when I cried it was for him and for me because I knew there could be no hope now for either of us. It was the end.

I slipped in and out of turbulent and terrifying nightmares and was no longer conscious of the passing of time or of cold or of hunger. Lin, Uncle Sung, the lama and a pack of ravenous golden wolves peopled these nightmares and recurrent in all of them was my yeti – 'Red' I called him – who saved us all time and time again. I had been fending off the wolves with my staff and I was about to be torn apart when Red came bounding across the snow and drove them off. I was not at all surprised at this for he had done it often enough before – he always seemed to arrive just in time. He was bending over me asking if I was hurt when I noticed he was not alone. There were two of them peering into my face. Then they began to sniff and lick me from head to toe, and I didn't much care for that. The feel of their hot breath on my ear tickled me and I pushed them away and sat up, dreading as I did so the abandonment of my dreams and the return to the reality of my living nightmare. But it was no dream.

The two yetis sat back on their haunches in front of me and studied me closely. The first I recognised at once as the yeti I had come to know as Red in my dreams, but the second was clearly older. He was white about the head and beard. The skin of his face was darker, more heavily creased and more deeply etched with wrinkles. He seemed only to have one ear, though it was difficult to tell through the hair. His eyes glinted gold in the fire. They were talking to each other, or perhaps it was to me, for they never took their eyes off me. It was hardly a language as we know it, more a sequence of curious moans and whimpers, but nonetheless formed and deliberately intoned. It was not the insane hysterical chattering of a monkey that I was listening to, but considered speech, however unintelligible it might have been to me.

I looked from one to the other. The older yeti – for that is what I presumed the white hair indicated – reached out slowly and touched me on my hair. I had not realised until then how extraordinarily long their arms were. The hand was leathery on the inside and black, and the thumb was as long as the other fingers. I shrank back but the arm seemed to stretch out after me like elastic. The touch on my face was smooth and leathery. His eyes looked into mine and there was a gentleness that calmed me at once. He arranged his lips carefully, and then he spoke, "Leelee," he said, first to me and then to Red. "Leelee," and then both of them together. "Leelee," their voices high with excitement. "Leelee! Leelee!

Leelee!" It seemed a sound I could imitate, and so I talked back to them and ventured a smile. "Leelee," I said, surprised at the strength in my own voice. Smiles wreathed their faces, revealing jagged, discoloured teeth. It was then that Red noticed my ash effigy. For some moments they considered it seriously together and then broke into peals of screeching laughter, piling more and more ash on the stomach to make it fatter. Before I knew it Red had lifted me off my feet and was hugging me so tight that I had to struggle for breath. To fight against such strength would not have been possible anyway, but there seemed little reason to struggle against them because these were hugs of affection. They passed me from one to the other like a precious doll. It was as if they had to hug me to believe I was real. Satisfied at last that I was, they squatted down before the fire to warm themselves, looking across at me from time to time and uttering whimpers of delight. It was a few moments later before I realised they were not just warming themselves. There was a sudden sweet smell of roasting meat. Crouched over the fire the two yetis turned and prodded the hunk of meat that lay buried in the bed of red ashes. By the smell I supposed it to be mutton, but I did not care what it was. It seemed an eternity before they rolled it out onto the floor, wrenched it apart and offered it to me. "Voo," said the elder yeti or 'One Ear' as I now thought of him. "Voo. Voo." And we sat together in front of the fire silent over our meal.

I devoured mine like a mad creature, licking my

fingers until the last taste of meat was gone. No matter that it was burned on the outside and raw on the inside, no matter that I ate so fast I nearly choked. My gorging was watched with delight by the two yetis who imitated me licking my fingers. "Leelee," they cried. "Leelee!" And they set to hugging me all over again. So I thought little of it when some time later One Ear picked me up again. I braced myself as he hugged me, but then he dumped me on Red's back, and before I knew it I was outside the door, a rush of cold wind on my face and One Ear was bounding ahead on all fours through the snow.

As Red followed I clung on round his neck and gripped his sides with my knees. Twice in those first few yards I came off and tumbled into the snow. He laughed and waited for me to clamber on again before setting off after One Ear, springing almost immediately into a run. I curled my fingers into his hair, laid myself along the back of his neck and hung on like a leech. I had had a horse bolt under me once before and this was a similar experience, but after the first few minutes it was not so alarming since I felt Red wanted me to stay on. As my confidence grew I relaxed, and the flow and the rhythm of his legs under me became easier to anticipate and to ride. Until then I had been so busy trying not to fall off that I had not even thought about where they were taking me or why, and even now I was not that concerned about it. I only knew that they had found me and fed me, that they had greeted me like some long lost friend. I was elated perhaps by the speed at which we travelled, faster than any horse I had ever ridden, but more I think because I knew that my ordeal by hunger was at last over.

Every few minutes they would stop and I noticed they always slowed down together and came to a halt precisely at the same moment, seemingly without any signal or word passing between them. One Ear would rear up onto his back legs and lift his nose into the wind, while beneath me I could feel Red's body taut with concentration. For a few moments they would listen and watch, still as statues; and then the rocking journey would begin again. We climbed all that day, speeding effortlessly through the snow. The valley bottoms were hidden now under the clouds, and by that evening we had only the dark blue of the sky above us. We were, it seemed, travelling on top of the world, and the yetis kept up this relentless pace, stopping less frequently now. My hands and fingers were so numb by this time that only the failing strength of my arms kept me from sliding off. My legs were quite useless below the knees. I had nothing to grip with. Red seemed to sense this for from time to time he would stop and a great arm would reach out from under me and arrange me so that my balance was restored.

As dark came on we had left the peaks above us and were making a slow and difficult descent across rock-strewn glaciers. Crevasses and chasms that looked impassable we leapt with consummate ease. Then we were in amongst sparse pine trees that clung impossibly to the mountainside and as the last of the light vanished we were swallowed quite suddenly by a dense forest that shut out the last of the day.

We stopped and I let myself down gently for I could not feel my feet as they touched the ground. There was a hurried hushed conversation between One Ear and Red and then to my astonishment I saw One Ear climb high into the tree beside us and swing away through the canopy of the trees until I could see him no more. I thought for one terrible moment as Red picked me up that we would follow him, but instead, with Red clasping me to his chest with one arm and my legs wrapped around him, we moved slowly through the undergrowth. It was the most painful part of the journey. Twigs and branches tore at me so that to protect myself I buried my face in Red's chest and closed my eyes.

It was some hours later when at last he stopped and set me down on my feet. I could see we were in a small clearing. There was the smell of wood smoke in the air and excited whispers from somewhere ahead of us in the darkness. Red led me along a path beside a black cliff face and then I saw a flickering glow emerging from the cliff some distance away. "Leelee!" Red called out beside me. "Leelee!" And then One Ear was there in front of us, his face lit up. He held out his hand, and so with Red on one side and One Ear on the other I was led in through the mouth of the cave. The strong light dazzled me at first. I could make out many figures, perhaps a dozen or more running towards us. A great fire in the centre revealed a vast cavern which seemed to stretch back into the cliff as far as the eye could see. I felt myself hoisted suddenly up onto Red's shoulders as the crowd of yetis rushed towards us. "Leelee!" they chanted. "Leelee!" And every one of them it seemed wanted to touch some part of me. My hands and knees were squeezed and patted, my fingers prised apart, examined and smelt. I could see that many of them had tears in their eyes.

Each one of them was different. There were a few with tawny, rust coloured hair, but none were the colour of 'Red'. Many had a greyer coat. It was clear at once that there were several old ones amongst them for they were white around the face like One Ear – and it was in particular these older yetis that seemed overcome, almost ecstatic at my arrival. I felt famous. I felt adored. The young yetis, some of them even smaller than me, were plucked from their mothers and held up to touch me, but most of these were terrified and screamed to be put down, much it seemed to everyone else's amusement.

Then I noticed one young yeti who had fallen in beside us and was walking with us now, his hand in Red's. He was looking up at me, but his was no adoring look. Instead there was a cold glare in his eyes that forced me to turn away. He was almost the same colour as Red and I thought of them at once as father and son. They were too alike to be otherwise. One Ear stood on a rock in the centre of the cave, his back to the fire, and made a speech, not a word of which I could understand of course, save the

53

word that I took by now to be the name by which they knew me, "Leelee". He kept pointing to a crudely fashioned, four-legged stool beside him on the rock. A chorus of raucous shrieking heralded a ceremony that I can only describe as a kind of coronation.

Almost solemnly One Ear took my hand and helped me up onto the rock. He led me towards the stool. It was clear I was expected to sit. As I did so a thunderous cheer went up. I thought then of the lama's 'mo', that I should one day soon be a king, 'king of the cloud forests', and I wished that Uncle Sung could be with me to witness it.

The seat of the stool beneath me was solid enough but I felt the legs were loose. It wobbled precariously. I could see no other piece of furniture in the cave and was wondering how it came to be there when Red approached me holding in his hands a small painted tin. There were faces on the outside of it, faces I thought I recognised but could not identify. A sudden silence fell on the cave. They were waiting for me to do something. I could think of nothing else but to reach down and take the box that he seemed to be offering to me. I put it down on my knees. There was writing on it. 'E.A.' in large letters, and then 'Coronation King Edward VII and Queen Alexandra. One Shilling'. I opened it. It was empty, except for an old photograph, a knife with a bone handle and a briar pipe.

"Leelee!" They cried. "Leelee! Leelee!" I smiled at them and held up the tin. This appeared was the proper response for the cheering broke out again. Looking around me I saw only one of them was not ecstatically happy. 'Little Red', as I called him, stood by his father and looked straight into my eyes. It was a look of naked hatred.

6

My bed that night was not unlike the hospital beds back at the Mission, made as it was of wooden supports but stretched across with skins rather than canvass. Like the yetis around me on the floor of the cave, I slept under a wolfskin rug that tickled my chin. The coronation tin had been taken from me and set on the rock ledge in the wall just above my bed, but it was the photograph inside that troubled me. That photograph was enough to keep me awake for most of the night. The faces that looked out at me had set my mind racing. It was mottled with damp spots, but clearly discernible were the faded brown figures of a mother, a father and a young man – their son I supposed. The parents were elegantly dressed, but in old fashioned clothes, the father with a high, stiff collar and a long jacket and the mother in a tightly waisted, full-length dress that seemed to be gathered up behind her somehow. Her face was obliterated by a damp spot, but the father looked proud and supercilious, his chin held high. It was the young man though that both troubled me and interested me most. He was wearing a strange kind of clerical cassock, not unlike my father's, except that there were buttons down the middle, a low slung belt and white bands on his throat, just like father used to wear at the Mission chapel on Sundays. The bands must have blown up to touch his chin at just the moment the photograph was taken. His face was, I felt, trying not to smile and only just succeeding, and there was something familiar about this face that struck me at once. There could be no doubt at all that there was some resemblance between this young man and myself – although he looked older than I. Written across the bottom of the photograph in copperplate hand-writing were the words: "With Mama and Papa. C.H.".

I lay there all night struggling in vain to puzzle out the endless questions that seemed to have no satisfactory answers. That I was known by the yetis in some way was obvious. It could be, I thought, that they were even expecting me. After all they even had a name for me. With the exception of Little Red I was, it seemed, universally loved, indeed I was almost revered by the older ones. It was clear to me that they thought I had been here before. What was quite certain was that someone had been here before me. How else could the coronation tin, the knife, the pipe and the photograph have got here? It was possible they had been stolen of course, but why? And where did the bed and the stool come from? Who did they belong to? And what was the significance of the coronation tin, anyway? The niche in the rock above my bed that housed the box was filled with flowers almost as if it was some kind of shrine. The young man in the photograph was the only positive clue I had. Who he was and why he was important I could not know. All I could assume was that the yetis believed him to be me and me to be him, that I had inherited his position amongst them, that of a king or a priest perhaps.

Such thoughts kept me awake for many hours that night. Beyond the fire I could see the silhouettes of two yetis squatting by the entrance beyond the fire, and from somewhere deep in the blackness of the cave came the occasional bleating of a sheep. I lay in the dark thinking only of Uncle Sung who had brought me so far and through so many dangers, but try as I did I could not picture the reassuring smile I knew and loved so well – and how I yearned for it now. Instead I could see only his body lying stiff in the snow and the wolves circling. I tried to thrust that terrible nightmare from my mind, but nothing, not even the lama's 'mo' could take its place. I wept silently in an agony of grief and loneliness, biting the sleeve of my coat to stop myself from crying out loud. I had lost the dearest friend I had and I was alone in the world.

The sheep woke me in the morning as the yetis drove them noisily past me towards the mouth of the cave. Some of the smallest yeti children bounded over towards me as I got up and then sat back on their haunches to consider me at a safe distance until they were called away. They scampered off after the sheep, herding them like sheepdogs and looking back at me from time to time over their shoulders. The sheep were proving awkward and obstinate and refused to be driven out of the cave, their leaders baulking and stamping their hooves. They were thickset, short-legged creatures with spindly horns, except for the sturdiest of the flock, a ram I took him to be, who boasted a pair of handsome curled horns which he tossed threateningly at the yeti children as they herded him towards the cave mouth. Panic-stricken lambs bolted in and out of the flock bleating for their mothers. There was bedlam in the cave as the last of the wayward sheep was rounded up and driven out, shepherded by an escort of screeching yetis.

Red, One Ear and a few others stayed behind squatting by the fire. As I came over to them One Ear took my arm and hugged me to him. I was offered a place between Little Red and his father. They were scooping milk one-handed from a dip in the rock. This I found very difficult to imitate, but they encouraged me to do so and looked puzzled at my ineptitude. More often than not my hand would arrive empty at my mouth but I was just beginning to master this enough to satisfy my thirst when I felt myself jolted sideways and most of the milk went in my ear or down my neck. When I glanced at Little Red I knew for sure it had been no accident. The yetis were all looking at me, waiting to see what I would do. I felt it was a kind of challenge that I could not ignore. Little Red leaned forward to scoop his milk. I waited for the right moment and jolted his arm as he raised it to his lips. Little Red lost most of the milk in his beard, and he turned on me his teeth bared. The yetis squealed with delight. Clearly I had done what was expected of me. I thought then he would launch himself at me and leapt to my feet to be ready, but Red grabbed his arm and held him back. Little Red's eyes glared into mine momentarily before he resumed his drinking in sullen silence. I had made an enemy amongst the yetis.

That first day living with the yetis was to tell me much about how they lived. With many of the yetis gone away into the forest, I supposed to shepherd the sheep, those that remained gathered round the fire. There followed a debate to which I listened trying to glean some vestige of meaning, but I failed. There was no apparent leader, but it was clear that when One Ear spoke the others listened attentively. Even more respected, I soon discovered, was the most ancient looking yeti I called 'White Beard', who sat silent by the fire during the debate, a great grey wolfskin wrapped around him. He was entirely covered in white whispy hair, his eyes almost hidden under thick white brows. His silence was commanding. Though he said little, it was immediately apparent to me that his approval was sought for everything – with the yetis it seemed that age was much respected.

The older yetis stayed behind in the cave whilst the young ones dispersed in ones and twos. I thought, indeed I hoped that I might be left behind with One Ear and White Beard, but clearly there was some competition between the yetis as to who should take me with them. That much I could understand. I was still feeling weak from my privations. Though I could feel no pain, I could see my left foot was still swollen and not fit to walk on. I could still feel nothing below my ankles. The frost seemed to have set in my feet and would not leave. In the end it fell to Red to take my hand and lead me out of the cave and of course I could not refuse. They would not understand my excuses and anyway I felt somehow they expected me to want to go. They seemed to assume I knew where I was going and what for.

Outside I was hoisted on to Red's back and with Little Red running or swinging ahead of us through the trees we left the light of the clearing and plunged into the forest. I had to learn quickly the knack of dodging and ducking under the branches, and I envied the ease with which Little Red flew above us through the trees.

I heard the roar of the river long before I saw it. Little Red was already waiting for us squatting on a boulder above a rushing waterfall that fell into a series of deep green pools. Red lowered me to the ground and took my hand. Little Red sprang from his boulder and ran across to us as we came out of the trees. He pushed me violently to one side and took Red's hand in his, looking up at him lovingly. It was only then that I realised the source of his antipathy towards me. I was never, his eyes warned me, never to come between him and his father if I knew what was good for me. Of all the yetis, Little Red was the only one I felt posed any threat to me, so I determined not to fuel his jealousy and to stay away from Red if it was at all possible. But the damage had been done as I was to find out all too soon.

I thought at first we had stopped at the river only to drink. The two yetis crouched down on all fours on the bank their mouths close to the water, but they made no attempt to drink. In time Little Red moved away from his father and walked up-river where he lay down full length on a flat boulder that hung out over a pool. He had his nose in the water. He had one hand steadying himself on the bank beside him, the other was dangling in the river. There was no violent thrashing of the water, no great excitement as Little Red caught his first fish and threw it casually up in the air beside him to let it gasp to death on the bank. It was a sizeable fish too – Lin would have turned ten cartwheels in celebration of a fish like that. Perhaps Little Red was in a better place than his father for he was catching much more often and they were always bigger. They looked like a species of brown speckled trout. I didn't like watching them die slowly so I took a stone and did the killing much as I used to do with Lin – a sharp tap on the back of the neck was all that was needed to finish them.

Red turned and beckoned me over towards him, urging me to come quietly as I came. He was pointing down into the water, so I let myself down slowly and peered over the edge. The fish seemed almost to be queueing up to be caught in the shallows below me. Most were too small to bother with but in amongst them was a monster of a fish that swam motionless against the flow of the river. Red took my hand and lowered it gently into the water. With his hand on mine I stroked the fish along the ridge of its back. The other fish seemed to know what might soon happen and vanished one by one. Before I knew it and before the fish knew it Red had it by the tail and it was flying high in the air back on to the grass behind us. I scrambled after it, but it squirmed out of my hands time and again before at last I had a firm grip on it. I was looking around for a stone to kill it with when a shadow fell over me. I looked up. Little Red was standing over me. He bent down, snatched the fish out of my hands and bowled it over my head towards the river. It fell short and lay in the grass flapping feebly.

Everything happened very fast after that. That he was challenging me yet again was obvious to me, and the coward in me which is never very far from the surface told me to ignore it, to turn the other cheek. I got to my feet and turned away from him. The moment I did so I sensed it was the wrong thing to have done. With a snarl he was on my back and I was falling forwards and rolling. I tried to protect my face with my hands but I had no other defence – I could feel the terrible strength of his arms around me. I struggled only to escape, not to fight back. I heard Red cry out and then we were in the sudden cold of the river together and sinking. I felt the water come in my mouth and nose. The grip on my neck faltered and I broke free. I kicked upwards towards the light, choking convulsively and sucking in more water as I fought for breath. Then I was breathing air instead of water and saw that I was only a few yards from the bank. My feet found rock and I was scrambling out of the water and Red was dragging me clear.

On all fours I coughed the river water out of my lungs and fought for my breath. When I looked up Red was gesticulating violently and screeching. I turned in time to see Little Red disappear beneath the surface, a red shadow beneath the water and drifting slowly towards the waterfall at the bottom of the pool. Red kept stepping into the water and coming back out again whining pathetically. I could not understand why he did not go in after his son. I saw Little Red's arms clutching at the air and then I realised that neither of them could swim.

"Leelee!" Red cried, his eyes beseeching. He was pulling at my arm dragging me down towards the river. "Leelee!" I pulled off my sodden coat and my boots and dived into the river. I had no fear of the water – I had Lin to thank for that – but I felt the cold numbing me and slowing me as I swam. Little Red seemed to move away from me as fast as I could swim, and it was only because he was swept round and round in the eddying water that I managed to reach him before the waterfall took him. I caught him round the neck under the crook of my arm and turned for the bank. He was a dead weight and for a few dreadful moments I felt myself useless against the force of the water. The current was taking us inexorably towards the roar of the waterfall. It must have been the panic in me that gave strength to my tired legs and I kicked furiously for the bank. Red ventured knee-deep into the pool to haul us in and then I was sitting stunned by the cold watching Little Red spluttering face down on the grass beside me.

Red carried his half-conscious son back through the forest and I ran along behind trying to stamp the life back into my legs and feet. Once back in the cave Little Red and I sat side by side covered in wolfskins as the great fire shivered the warmth back into us and gave us feeling again. My feet tingled to life, the first sensation I had had in them for days. The story seemed to spread backwards through the cave bringing everyone running to the fire to hear more. The she-yetis left off milking the sheep and the children raced around the fire shrieking with excitement until White Beard cuffed one of them and they settled down to listen to Red's story again.

The children who just this morning had hardly dared approach me came and squatted by me and patted me and stroked me. Little Red sat silent and sullen throughout all this, hanging his head. At last he was called before White Beard who stood beside me on the speaking rock and who berated him formally in front of everyone. The matter seemed to be over.

There was a meal of fish, honey and milk and then One Ear stood up on the speaking rock and I was invited to sit up beside him on the rickety stool that had become my throne. Red took the coronation tin off its shelf and handed it to me reverently. Then he went and sat down with the others. Everyone was looking up at me with great expectancy on their faces. They seemed to want me to speak and so I did. "Leelee!" I said, putting my hand on my chest.

"Leelee!" they echoed.

"Man," I said – it was all I could say that I thought they might understand.

"Maa," they cried.

I pointed at them: "Yeti."

"Yay, yay, yay," they chorused. They had done this before, of that I was quite sure. They were all insatiably eager to learn, even the children, but it was the older yetis who seemed to find the words easier to pronounce, almost I felt as if they knew them already and might be teasing me. Whether or not this was true they clearly possessed phenomenal powers of concentration and memory as well as a determined wish to learn. The lesson went on until One Ear called a halt – by that time I had taught them every part of the body I could properly point to and we all left the fire and went away to our beds.

I was halfway into my sleep when a touch on my cheek brought me back out of it. "Leelee," said a voice. The dark silhouette could have been almost any of them. I sat up on my elbows. The face turned so that the light from the fire flickered across it. It was Little Red. He reached out and touched my cheek again. "Leelee," he said, and then he was gone. My enemy had become my friend.

7

When I look back now on my early months amongst the yetis I am often puzzled at how quickly I became one of them. After the fight with Little Red and our reconciliation I was never again made to feel afraid of any of them. On the contrary, they each claimed me and protected me rather enviously. I was for ever being picked up and carted off to be groomed and cosseted. I felt cocooned in the warmth of their affection and secure in my honoured position, though precisely how they saw me I was not at all sure. Sometimes I was a plaything or a mascot, then a teacher and then a king – it seemed to change from day to day, from hour to hour even. But whatever I was to them I knew I was safe amongst them.

I suppose my easy assimilation into their band can also be put down to the fact that I had no alternative but to make the best of things. I was after all obliged to stay with my hosts. Very early on I thought of escaping, not because I was unhappy – though the loss of Uncle Sung preyed terribly on my mind – but because I knew it was not my world, that I did not belong. But where should I go to and what for? On my own I would have had little chance of survival in the forest beyond the cave and still less in the mountains beyond. Uncle Sung was dead, and my father thousands of miles away in China, so far away as to be unreal to me – and anyway he too might well be dead by now. So I never really considered the matter of escape very seriously. That may seem strange, but when you are young you live for the present so long as you are content, and the longer I stayed the more contented I became. I was amongst a people who clearly loved me. They fed me, and they kept me warm. What more could I want?

My only fear was that I might be found out, that when the time came I might not be able to do what was expected of me, whatever that might be. I often looked at the face of the young priest in the photograph and examined the coronation tin minutely, but I could find no clue in either to help me. It was a chocolate tin – that much I knew from the writing I found indented on the bottom: 'Cadbury Bros. Ltd.'. From the reverence with which they treated it, I felt that the tin must have some magical property associated with learning, for it was always in the evenings that they brought it to me on the speaking rock. Perhaps they perceived the coronation tin as the source of my teaching power. I could not tell. But with or without the coronation tin I was admired and adored. Even so I felt I was expected to be as they were, to live as they did, and so I slipped as far as I could into their yeti ways.

Language was never a barrier between us, for much of the communication between them was by touch or by sign. As I got to know them I could read more clearly what they were thinking and feeling from their facial expressions, which were not dissimilar to ours but more varied and exaggerated. Unlike us they use their eyes rather than their mouths to communicate and since no yeti ever hides his feelings, it was not long before I was able to understand each of them well enough. If there were any difficulties they delighted in using the few words I was teaching them. They could not, I soon discovered, manage words of more than one sound; and hard consonants were unpronounceable to them, so 'water' was 'waa', 'milk' became 'mil' or 'milmil' and food, 'voo'.

Of them all Little Red learned the fastest, because I suppose he was almost constantly with me. And I was grateful for his companionship. He often rescued me from the clutches of one of the more maternal she-yetis and took me away to fish by the river. Even at night now he would leave his father's side and come and curl up foetus-like beside my bed. It was mostly from Little Red that I learned how to live as yetis live. I did what he did as far as that was possible. Although I was about the same height as Little Red I could run at only half his speed, and I just did not possess the strength or flexibility in my arms to climb the trees and swing from branch to branch as he did. But he understood that as indeed they all did. He helped me as if I was a toddler learning to walk. Within the limits of my feeble, hairless body, I was learning to be one of them.

Little yetis, I soon discovered, squabble and fight much as we do as children, and are every bit as mischievous and disobedient. They have a great talent for practical jokes. Ambush is a favourite ploy. They would scoot up a tree and drop like a stone on some unsuspecting passer by and then scamper off screeching before anyone could catch them. In spite of my privileged position amongst them I was often the victim of their ambushes and each time it knocked the breath out of me – yeti children are never small. If Little Red was with me, as he often was, he would catch up with the culprit and swing him round his head before releasing him to stagger off giddy and wailing back to the cave where little sympathy was shown. Favourite too was feather tickling. Many a time I lay and watched them first thing in the morning. They would creep up on some slumbering yeti (never Red, One Ear or White Beard I noticed) and with a long feather proceed to tickle the hands, feet and nostrils until the unfortunate yeti stirred and then woke with a furious roar like the fee-fi-fo-fum giant of the nursery books. By this time the villainous little yeti had made good his escape and had vanished into the darkness at the back of the cave.

In all there were twenty four yetis living together in the cave, the she-yetis slightly smaller in stature than the males, their faces finer-boned, their eyes rounder and larger under less heavy brows. Other-wise, covered as they were in long hair, male and female were difficult to tell apart. I never did manage to work out exactly which children belonged to which parents. With some, like Little Red, it was obvious enough, but not with most. Once weaned from their mothers the little yetis seemed to belong to everyone.

Some of the older yetis were more popular than others with the children – it depended I suppose on their patience threshhold. White Beard they kept well clear of and I noticed they were wary too of One Ear. It seemed that Red was quite happy to be clambered over by several little yetis at a time. But there were two adult yetis in particular, 'Auntie' and 'Uncle' I called them, who took the brunt of communal parenting on themselves, and to whom the children invariably went when they were in trouble. It was always to Auntie and Uncle too that everyone looked when childish rages spilled over into violent quarrels. This was rare enough, and always terrifying to me.

I saw more fights over sticks than anything else, the worst being a furious struggle between 'Bowlegs', a somewhat sullen little yeti who rolled from side to side as he walked, and 'Digger', a solitary sort who would spend much of his day digging for grubs and worms outside the cave. Bowlegs had a passion for sticks, particularly if they belonged to someone else – he kept a hoard of them in the cave and guarded them jealously. I don't know how it began, but I suspect Bowlegs must have tried to steal Digger's digging stick. The first I heard of it was a crescendo of frenzied screeching outside the cave. I looked up to see them fighting tooth and claw and rolling in the mud. It took both Red and One Ear to pull them apart and they were dragged back into the cave. Auntie and Uncle tried to calm them down and to reconcile them, but they were still seething with fury when White Beard called them to the speaking rock. Uncle presented him with Digger's broken stick – as evidence I suppose – and explained what had happened. They both gave their side of the story, before White Beard publicly admonished them. Bowleg's collection of sticks was brought from the back of the cave and laid at White Beard's feet. He pointed to the fire. Reluctantly, but without a murmur, Bowlegs picked them up and threw them on the fire, all of them except one which White Beard gave to Digger. Bowlegs sulked after that and was comforted by Auntie and Uncle who stayed with him constantly, forever grooming him and playing with him. Two days later I looked out of the cave and saw Bowlegs crouched down beside Digger and digging in the same hole. He sat back on his haunches and held out a worm to Digger who took it and ate it and bent to the digging again. Forgiveness seemed to be an elemental part of their nature.

The daylight hours were spent in a constant search for food, a search in which everyone played his part, even the little yetis, even me. I shepherded the sheep through the forest to the clearings on the scree slope

73

and stood guard over them with Little Red and the yeti children whilst the she-yetis vanished into the forest to return some time later, their leather sacks bulging with snails, nuts and mushrooms. I fished the river with Little Red so that I knew where the fish lay in each pool, and which pools the fish preferred – this seemed to depend on how close they were to the hot spring which bubbled up near the river some distance upstream, and how shaded the pools were by the overhanging trees. The warmer and darker the water the better they seemed to like it. I milked the sheep and hung up the mushrooms to dry over the fire. I dug for roots in the forest around and gathered berries in their thousands.

In all these tasks except one, I found myself inept, too weak or too small. I discovered however that I could drive the sheep better than any of them, for I could whistle. The sheep moved along a great deal faster for me than they did for the yetis. This was something that gave me much satisfaction, and also brought me much esteem amongst the yetis who tried in vain to imitate me.

The hunt for food was fruitful until the winter came. By then they had collected a vast store of nuts and dried mushrooms, which they kept in deep holes dug into the floor at the back of the cave. The lambs would be killed and eaten more often now and the whole band became even more heavily reliant on the sheep. There was less milk to be had, for the grazing was poor on the slopes. They often had to dig away the snow by hand to enable the sheep to graze at all.

Indeed all the food had to be eked out through the dark months, the older yetis rationing the nuts and dried mushrooms – no one could take more in a day than they could carry in their cupped hands.

I remember well the dark winter evenings around the fire with the sheep roasting over the flames. The yetis would sing while they squatted together waiting for the meat to cook. I can best describe the sound as a throbbing drone, made through their noses, with mouths closed, the eyes fixed intently on the meat as it dripped its fat into the fire. They rose and fell on their haunches in perfect time, their hands beating their thighs. The drone rose in pitch and volume until the moment came when the meat was at last pulled apart and handed out. The liver I noticed always went to the males and the heart to pregnant or suckling females. They ate the meat in silence, licking their fingers until not a taste of it was left.

Such a feast always followed a hunt. I presumed at first that the yeti hunted the wolf for its skin which was indeed warmer than sheepskin, but as I was to discover later this was not the only reason. Only the adult males went out after the wolf and then only in pairs or groups, never alone. Even Little Red had not yet been allowed to go. Whenever Red went off hunting Little Red would pester him to be taken and would sulk for hours when he was left behind. They carried no weapons but few hunting parties returned empty-handed. The return of the hunters would be an occasion for great celebration, the wolf skin always being presented to White Beard who, watched by the entire band, would himself scrape the hide clean with a sharpened flint and peg it out by the fire. The triumphant hunter would take his place on the speaking rock and tell his story of the hunt. Of course I never understood exactly what had happened, but from their gestures I gathered that they killed the wolves either by lying in ambush for them and dropping onto them out of the trees, or sometimes there was a long chase, but both methods ended the same way with a sharp twist to the neck. This dénouement was always accompanied by screeches of delight, the children cavorting in wild excitement. The cooking of the sheep would follow and the drone song, the sound of which I can still hear to this day throbbing in my ears.

Perhaps they learnt the drone song from the bees whose honey was the yeti's greatest delicacy. The discovery of a honeycomb hanging precariously high on a cliff face sent ripples of anticipation through the yeti band. It took some time for them to calm down and gather round the speaking rock. The younger yetis saw it I think as a great challenge, a kind of public proving. Each volunteer in turn, and there was never a shortage, would take his place on the speaking rock and lay his or her claim to the climb – that is what I assumed anyway. If I understood right, and the longer I stayed the more I did, the discoverer of the honeycomb had a prior claim. When everyone had had their say it was left to White Beard to decide.

Yetis are wondrously agile swinging amongst the trees. They seem to be able to defy gravity, but on a cliff face they have the same difficulties as we do. The cliffs were often wet and slippery and the footholds and handholds few and far between. Accidents did happen. I was witness to several, many of which could have been fatal but for the yetis natural ability to land on their feet. But once even this extraordinary acrobatic talent was not enough.

I could sense the anxiety around me one spring morning as we watched a young she-yeti called 'Shoo' begin her climb. I had my own names for all the yetis by now, some of them not at all flattering. Shoo sneezed often, and noisily. She was a messy creature, always scratching herself with energetic enthusiasm, rubbing bald patches on her sides. She even sneezed in her sleep. She was darker than most of the yetis, a dull, mud brown, and had spent a lot of time I noticed following Little Red, who ignored her – whether deliberately or not I couldn't tell.

It was a long way up the cliff face to the honeycomb – indeed I could hardly see it – but Shoo made her way easily enough at first along a series of narrow ledges. From the bottom of the cliff came a chorus of encouragement and advice in even amounts, all the advice coming from the older yetis. Then halfway up everyone fell silent and watched. It was difficult to see against the sunlight and Shoo was dark, almost the same colour as the rock. She inched her way upwards, sometimes having to traverse the rock downwards it seemed to me in order to find a safe route up to the honeycomb. She was as high as the treetops, but still a long way from the honeycomb when she simply fell away from the face of the cliff. There was no cry as she came down, arms and legs outspread, turning over and over in the air. She fell through the brittle branches of a tree that grew at the foot of the cliff and hit the ground only a few paces away from me.

She lay still, one arm twisted beneath her and there was blood on her lips. Auntie, Uncle and One Ear were beside her at once and trying to shake her back to life. No one else moved. Suddenly I was aware that they were all looking at me.

"Leelee," said White Beard, taking my arm and leading me to where Shoo lay. When yetis cry they moan tremulously. All around me I saw grief-stricken faces, hope and faith written on every one of them. The yeti at my feet lay broken and still as the dead. I understood now what they wanted of me and what they expected of me and I knew I was bound to fail them. I was no healer. Of course I had watched Uncle Sung and Father at work at the Mission hospital often enough, but I had no medical skill whatsoever, no real knowledge of how the human body worked or how to heal it. They would discover now at last that the young priest in that photograph and I were not one and the same. There was nothing else I could do but to act out my part as best I could and hope for a miracle. So I knelt down and played doctor, touching Shoo on her forehead. At that moment her head turned and she groaned softly. There was instant relief and rejoicing amongst the yetis. One Ear lifted her up and carried her at the head of the procession back to the cave. As we walked back I felt Little Red put his arm round my neck as he always did when he wanted to show his loyalty and affection.

They laid Shoo by the fire and turned to me for instructions. I had none. They waited. I looked down at the yeti, who was bleeding from her mouth, and said a silent, secret prayer to the God of my father, the God I had turned away from and ignored for so long. I knelt down beside Shoo, my eyes closed. When I opened them a moment later Red was standing in front of me. He was holding the coronation tin out to me. "Leelee," he said. And all around me the yetis settled down on their haunches to watch and wait.

8

I remember exactly the moment I stopped merely pretending to be a doctor and began to think like one. I had been kneeling for some time at Shoo's side, my mind empty of solutions. I could feel they were already becoming worried and puzzled at my inactivity. Little Red was beside me, looking at me and waiting. One Ear and White Beard looked at each other. I could read doubt in their eyes. Little Red put his arm around me, but I dared not look at him and meet his eyes for they would be full of trust. I did not want to see his eyes clouding with disappointment and disillusion.

In my awkwardness I must have shifted on my knees for the coronation tin slipped off my lap and the lid fell open as it clattered to the ground. The photograph fluttered out and the pipe rolled out after it. There was a murmur of delight from all sides and that baffled me for I had done nothing and Shoo still lay inert and bleeding from the mouth. White Beard it was who reached forward and picked up the pipe. He gave it to me and I thought for a moment of putting it back in the tin, but from the reverence with which White Beard presented it to me I felt there must be a significance to the pipe which I should not ignore. I did the only other thing I could think of, and put it in my mouth. White Beard and the elders seemed delighted and settled down again to watch. The pipe in my mouth tasted musty and stale but I kept it there. One Ear took the knife from the tin and held the blade over the flames. Then, squatting down beside me, he offered it to me in both hands. I took it.

The young priest in the cassock looked up at me from the photograph on the ground. I hated him at that moment, cursing him for my hapless predicament. I brushed the ash off it, picked it up and laid it face down in the box, not wishing to be reminded of him any more. As I did so Shoo began to shiver convulsively. Suddenly now I knew what had to be done for I had seen this before back at the Mission hospital when the wounded Chinese soldiers were brought in. I did then what I had seen Uncle Sung and my father do a hundred times – indeed I had often been sent to fetch the blankets myself. She had to be kept warm at all costs. I laid out an under-blanket of several wolfskins close to the fire and folded a skin into a pillow for her. One Ear, who seemed naturally to adopt the role of my assistant, lifted the limp and senseless Shoo and lowered her gently onto it. I covered her then with skins until nothing was visible but her eyes and her mouth. I bathed her face with hot water and pinched her cut lip until the bleeding stopped. Then I sat cross-legged by her head, the knife like a sceptre in one hand. I chewed on my pipe and waited and hoped.

It seemed to take forever, but at last her teeth stopped rattling and she lay still again, breathing evenly. I knew well enough that if her neck or her back had been broken in the fall, then this would be the sleep that would end sooner or later in death. I tried to put that dreadful thought out of my mind but found it impossible to do so. Once I was sure she was warmed through I set about discovering as best I could whether or not she had broken any bones. I remembered the arm twisted hideously behind her back after she fell. I handed the knife to One Ear who never left my side and I ran my hands slowly over her legs and arms, but could feel nothing broken. I tipped her head sideways and felt the back of her neck. The neck seemed to move normally. The last thing I checked were her collar bones and I only did that because I remembered Lin had broken one of his when he had leapt once too often out of a tree by the river. He had walked around like a wounded soldier for weeks with his arm in a sling Uncle Sung had made for him. And sure enough the bone below her right shoulder had separated – I could feel the gap between. So I did exactly as Uncle Sung had done. I made a sling, out of leather it was, and tied it around her neck to hold the arm and shoulder in place. I had done all I could. There was nothing for it now but to wait, wait and pray, and I did plenty of praying that night.

Several times during the next day Shoo stirred and groaned but her eyes remained steadfastly shut and she would sink back always into a deep sleep. Every time she moved – and I was a little heartened by the fact that she could – there was great excitement amongst the yetis but then a corresponding sense of disappointment when she did not wake. All that day they sat with me and watched over her, scarcely taking their eyes from her face. Their concentration was awesome. I was conscious of a yearning, communal will that was seeking to drag her back to life. The children, some of whom moaned continuously with grief, were finally taken away by Auntie and busied themselves collecting wood for the fire. No one ate, no one spoke and no one slept.

The vigil went on through that evening and into the night. My hopes faded as the long hours passed and her breathing became shallow and irregular. Once I thought she had stopped breathing altogether and panic gripped me as the yetis all turned to me for reassurance. It was the only time, I think, that they doubted the outcome. I smiled weakly, sucked on my pipe and hoped. She breathed again but it was a rasping, ominous breathing and I prepared myself for the worst. I felt Little Red's arm come around my neck and twiddle the lobe of my ear – yetis have no lobes and Little Red in particular was fascinated with mine. I looked at him now, and I could see he was still happy, still secure in the knowledge that I was there with my coronation tin and my pipe and my knife and that all would somehow be well after all. I suppose this blind faith in Leelee and his powers must have been infectious because in spite of all the evidence now to the contrary I still dared hope that Shoo might yet wake and live.

But dawn brought a sharper sense of reality. In the thin light Shoo's eyes seemed to have sunk deeper in her face. The muscles in her cheeks and lips twitched and twisted, contorting her face horribly. The yetis took this for a sign of recovery and leaned closer waiting for her eyes to open. The breathing rattled in her throat and there was a long pause after each breath as if it were the last. I closed my eyes and prayed for her soul as I had so often seen my father do over a dying patient.

When I opened them I saw the lacy skeleton of a leaf had blown in and was caught in the hair above her forehead. I reached out to take it off and as I did so her eyes opened. Surprise and relief fused inside me and sent such a feeling of joy flooding through me that tears ran down my cheeks and into the corners of my mouth. Shoo looked around her from under heavy eyelids and then saw us and knew us. She struggled to sit up but hadn't the strength. But for everyone around the fire the miracle was clearly complete enough. Little Red hugged me so tight that he hurt me and the chant echoed through the cave: "Leelee! Leelee! Leelee!" Shoo looked up at me in bewilderment, scratched herself on her head and then sneezed explosively. She cried out and clutched her shoulder. I laughed then and bent down to help her to her feet. She staggered and yelped with pain as her arm settled into her sling. All the yeti children hooked up their arms across their chests and went wobbling and yelping round the fire until White Beard rose and the happy hysteria died. He picked up the tin, closed the lid and gave it to me solemnly, before putting his arms around me. Until that moment White Beard was the only yeti who had never embraced me. I felt honoured and humbled.

We feasted that night on mutton and milk and I drifted off to sleep with the coronation tin in my arms and the pipe, my healing pipe, clutched in my hand. I slept fitfully, waking every few hours to wonder about the pipe and the knife, and about that face in the photograph. Perhaps the yetis were right, perhaps there was a power inside the tin or did it lie solely in the pipe. And what did the knife signify? I hadn't used it except to cut the leather for the sling. I tossed the possibilities back and forth. Something had brought Shoo back from the dead, and most certainly it was not me.

My esteem amongst the yetis was high enough before Shoo's miraculous recovery, but now I became almost a God, a Messiah to them. I was not simply adored – I had always been that. I was beginning to be worshipped. I felt more and more that the speaking rock was becoming an altar to me and the coronation tin they brought me each evening before the teaching began took on the semblance of a sacrament.

But to my delight the children treated me as they had always done. To them I was still the easy butt for their practical jokes, for I was always taken by surprise and never fast enough in my reactions to administer the swift retribution they received from other yetis. They would mimic my upright walk and the delicate way I chewed my food – yetis do not chew their food as we do, they simply tear it apart and swallow it. One of them – I called him 'Tot' for he was the tiniest yeti in the cave – would sit by me and copy my every move. Although still feeding from his mother, he would seek me out wherever I was and tease me until I took some notice of him. Soon my shoulders became his favourite transport. He was not heavy but he would poke his fingers in my eyes and pull at my hair which by now had grown long and straggly. When his mother tried to take him back for feeding, Tot would cling to my leg like a limpet and Little Red had to help prise him away. He was also a terrible thief and particularly fond of my felt boots. Time and again I would find one of my boots gone and he would be discovered later curled up asleep and sucking on it. Clearly there was something delicious about the taste of my boots.

The adult yetis tried to protect me from the attentions of Tot and the young ones, but to be honest I did not want or need their protection. I found that kind of playful affection much easier to respond to than the new deification I was being subjected to by their elders. I was flattered by it I suppose to begin with, but soon I found it began to distance me from them. Only Little Red stayed unchanged towards me, still a warm friend, a loyal guardian and my constant companion. With him I passed my days fishing in the river. Under his tuition I became adept at tickling trout – Lin would have been proud of me I thought – though I lost many because I was never patient enough and often struck too early before the fish was thoroughly mesmerized.

Then one day when the fish were not there to be caught and I became bored with the waiting I took off my clothes and walked slowly down into the water and began to swim. Little Red screeched in alarm as I swam out across the pool towards the far bank. He was watching me rigid with terror and I determined then that I would teach him how to swim, to show him that water could be mastered. I splashed and dived and rolled, and then lay floating on my back to show him there was nothing to fear. He came to the water's edge and crouched down to help me out. It took weeks after that to tempt him into the water. However, bit by bit I persuaded him that the water would hold him up if he would let it and he began to walk out deeper and deeper into the pool, and then at last took his feet off the bottom and let me hold him up. As with the learning of words, once a lesson was learned it was never forgotten, and within a few days all his fear was gone.

And so Little Red became the first yeti to learn how to swim and there was such delight on his face when he brought the whole band down one day to witness this new phenomenon. He took them completely by surprise. To everyone's consternation he leapt from a rock into the pool, sank, surfaced, shook the water off his face and then floundered frantically to the other side of the river and back. Auntie and Uncle screamed at him and Red implored me to go after him as I had done once before. Even White Beard who scarcely ever betrayed any anxiety, screamed at Little Red to come back, which he did in his own time. There was no panic in his floundering, only a lack of co-ordination, and Little Red was soon clambering out of the river in triumph and shaking himself like a dog over everyone.

The older yetis seemed to take this as further evidence, if any were needed, that I was indeed a worker of miracles, but all the same none of the adult yetis ever ventured into the water. Their fear of it was even more powerful it seemed than their belief in Leelee. But they trusted me enough to let the children come to the river, Tot amongst them.

To begin with they were all terrified and refused to put a foot in the water. No amount of cajoling and encouraging would persuade them. It was Shoo who took the first tentative step – as much to please Little Red as anything else I suspected. Soon the others followed her example and it was not long before most of them were swimming and frolicking in the river with Little Red. Only Tot stayed squatting resolutely on the bank. Nothing would induce him to come in. Weeks went by before he even allowed me to carry him in and then he clung trembling round my neck, gripping me so tight that I could scarcely breathe. I did not think he would ever let go of me, but as time passed he allowed me to bounce him up and down in the water and he began to enjoy kicking and splashing the water around him. And then one day, to my great delight and surprise, he launched himself clear of me and swam a few frantic strokes. It was the beginning. After that he found the promised buoyancy and very soon discovered he could speed through and under the water better than any of the others. He used this talent for making pike-like attacks on anyone unfortunate enough to be nearby, grabbing their legs and dragging them under – and all too often he picked me out as his quarry.

The older yetis, and in particular Auntie and Uncle, found it difficult to believe the evidence of their eyes and worried in spite of White Beard's repeated reassurances that if Leelee was there then all must be well. Auntie and Uncle never quite believed it. They hovered nervously on the bank clutching each other for comfort, but as the months passed they too came to enjoy the spectacle of Tot's acrobatic antics in the water, though even then they were always relieved when it was over.

On bright, clear days – and there were few enough of those in the forest – the river became a new gathering place for the band of yetis. They would build a great fire and bring down my stool and the coronation tin from the cave and I would sit with them by the warmth of the fire and teach them word lessons long into the evening, the tin always open on my lap, whilst exhausted yeti children curled up together by the fire to dry themselves. These were I think the happiest moments of my days amongst the yetis, but it was a happiness that was to prove shortlived.

I remember there was a terrible storm the night before it happened. The sound of the rain on the trees outside the cave had kept me awake all night. I think I knew the moment I opened my eyes that Tot was missing. It had become normal for him to come and sit on my chest to wake me up in the morning. He would prise open my eyelids with his sharp little fingers and peer into them to see if I was inside somewhere. Then satisfied that I was there he would jump up and down on me until he was quite sure I was fully awake or until someone dragged him off me. But that morning he did not come to wake me. I thought nothing more of it until I saw Tot's mother appear out of the darkness of the cave. Red was with her, his arm around her neck, and she was moaning quietly. Around the fire Uncle and Auntie looked distraught and White Beard and One Ear sat on their haunches staring grim-faced into the fire. Little guesswork was needed to interpret what Little Red was telling me as he squatted down beside me. I searched for my boots and could only find one of them.

I knew at once what had happened. If Tot was not inside the cave – and it seemed that had been searched thoroughly enough already – then he would be down by the river. Of that I was quite sure. I knew how often he had dragged me down there to watch him swim. I knew how he loved the water. I slipped unseen out of the cave and ran across the sunlit clearing into the forest beyond. The track to the river was downhill all the way and well trodden. I ran like the wind and as I came closer I shouted for him. The river was high and roaring, the water muddied. With growing relief I searched the bank and peered into the pools. I had been wrong. Thank God I had been wrong. He was not there after all. I was turning to go back to the cave when I spotted my boot lying in the grass under the shadow of a lichen-covered rock. I picked it up and cried out for him again and again until the forest echoed with his name.

"Leelee!" came the answer. "Leelee!" But it was not his voice. Little Red came running out of the forest. I just had time to push the boot into the pocket of my coat.

"No," I shouted, and shook my head vigorously. "No, not here. He's not here."

Little Red looked at me and I saw his shoulders sag as the hope went out of him. And I walked past him away from the river, torn inside with self-recrimination and grief.

9

Had I been thinking more clearly at the time and remembered the yetis' great capacity for forgiveness I am sure I should have brought myself to tell Little Red at once about the boot I had found by the river. Indeed as I ran back through the trees with Little Red I came close to confiding in him. Of all of them Little Red was the last I wanted to tell, but perhaps the only one I could tell.

I had little doubt that Tot had been washed away by the swollen river earlier that morning. He had no means of knowing that the placid pools where we had swum so often together could be transformed overnight by a storm, that the swirling currents would drag him down and sweep him over the waterfalls to his death. Had I not told them and shown them time and again how safe water was, how it would always cradle them and hold them up? Had I not done my level best to conquer their instinctive fear of the river? And who had been my best pupil, so quick to learn from me and trust me? Tot was lying drowned somewhere back there at the bottom of the river, and I alone was responsible. To search elsewhere would I knew be fruitless and would be a charade I could not act out.

Time and again I was about to tell Little Red but my courage failed me. Then I saw him drop to his knees on the track in front of me and put his nose to the ground. As soon as I caught up with him I saw it, a large dog-like print in the soft mud on the edge of the track. He looked up at me. "Ul!" he said quietly, and his eyes flickered nervously through the forest around us. It was a word I had taught them often round the fire as I held up a wolf skin. He was on his feet now, his face lifted to catch the scent. "Wolf?" I asked. "Is it a wolf then?"

"Ul, ul," he repeated, his eyes full of grief. I knew well enough by now how they feared wolves – I had always been surprised by the vehemence of their feelings whenever I held the wolfskin up during the word lessons from the speaking rock. But until now I had not realised either that the wolves penetrated so deep into the forest, nor that they ever attacked the yetis. I had imagined that the yetis were too strong and too fast to be threatened by any predator.

Little Red began to moan. I could see he had quite made up his mind that Tot was dead, that he had been carried off by a wolf. What need was there now for me to produce the boot? What was done was done, and there was no bringing him back. What matter that I knew it was the river that had taken him and not the wolves? What difference could that make now? How eagerly I grabbed the escape that had been offered me. How quickly and easily I justified my shabby cowardice. To my eternal shame I kept my silence and let a wolf take my place as Tot's killer.

News of Little Red's discovery did not at first seem to impress White Beard, who was the only one left in the cave by the time we got back. He squatted by the fire, morose and dismissive, as Little Red told him and pointed back into the trees. His reaction seemed to confirm what I had always thought, that wolves were their prey and not the other way round – there were enough skins around the cave to prove it. Perhaps he did not trust Little Red's judgement, or perhaps he was too stunned by sadness to think, I do not know. It was only when Red and One Ear appeared at the mouth of the cave shouting, "Ul! Ul!" that White Beard began to take notice. A few moments later Shoo came bounding towards us out of the forest, screeching for us to come. She pulled at Red's arm, trying to hurry him away. I could understand little of what she told us, but the dreadful urgency of it could not be mistaken.

Red threw me up onto his back and with White Beard scuttling along beside us, faster than I had ever seen him, we followed Shoo back into the forest. We had not far to go. The sound of bleating sheep should have warned me what to expect, but it did not. It was not until we came out of the trees and I saw the first scattering of wool and blood on the ground that I began to appreciate what had happened. Everything

I then saw and heard served to incriminate the wolves. There were a few sheep still surviving from the slaughter. They stood huddled together on the scree slope, penned around by the she-yetis, their children clinging around their necks. They faced outwards like defiant warriors on a battlefield defending their standard. All around them the hillside was littered with dead sheep, most with their throats torn out, lying on their sides or on their backs, legs in the air, their eyes staring heavenward. One look was enough to tell me that the flock had been decimated with barely half a dozen sheep still standing and some of those were terribly wounded. We listened as Auntie told the whole terrible story of how the she-yetis had left the flock to graze whilst they spread out through the forest to search for Tot. Details of course were lost to me, but I could picture from her dramatic gestures what must have happened. The pack of wolves had attacked and by the time the she-yetis had come running back the sheep had been scattered and the damage already done. All they could do was to drive the wolves off and round up the sheep that were left.

Everyone of them now believed Tot must have been taken by the same pack of marauding wolves. They had no reason to suspect anything else. The procession made its way slowly back along the narrow forest tracks like some defeated army, its soldiers drained of all spirit. I expected them to be roused to retribution, or at least to set out after the wolves to see if Tot was still alive. But no one even spoke. They were stunned by what had happened, and overwhelmed with sadness.

Around the fire that evening there was no appeal to Leelee to intervene on their behalf. They came to me only for consolation, and we hugged and stroked and groomed each other in mutual sympathy. Even Leelee it seemed could not bring Tot back, and they knew it. They understood the finality of death and accepted it. They grieved but they did not rage against it. No one called for revenge. On the contrary I think the raid only served to increase their fear and respect for their enemy. There was no tirade against the creatures that had murdered one of their own and massacred their sheep.

White Beard stood beside me on the speaking rock and addressed a solemn and attentive band. There was a sense of urgency about the meeting and much talk of 'milmil'. As he spoke I began to think that this was not the first time that the yetis or their sheep had been attacked by the wolves, and I understood now the significance of the wolf hunts and the triumphant celebration that had always followed a kill. Tot's death and the loss of their sheep was but one battle in an unending war of survival.

When he had finished there was no shortage of yetis to take his place on the speaking rock. One by one they came to the rock to volunteer just as the younger yetis had done before they climbed for the honeycombs. It became apparent that they had no intention of hunting down the wolves. It was sheep they were after, for unless they replaced their dead sheep there would be no milk and no meat.

It was Little Red who proposed I should go with them. He came over to where I was sitting on my stool and put his arm around me. There was some earnest debate about this, much of which was lost on me. I know that Auntie, amongst others, thought that it would safer for Leelee to stay behind with her and the children. She did not want me to go. But there was an immediate outcry at this. One Ear claimed that Leeelee would bring them good fortune. He held up the coronation tin and took out the knife and the pipe. I was sure he meant that its magic would save them if they were wounded. In the end I was amongst a dozen or so White Beard chose for the expedition.

We set off the next morning. In my drowsiness I forgot to take the coronation tin with me. I had already climbed up on Red's back when Tot's mother came running out of the cave, the tin in her hand. As she gave it to me her eyes were pleading and I had the fleeting but clear impression that she still harboured some hope that Tot might be alive, that by some miraculous power I might bring him back safely to her. It was at that moment as I looked down at her that I knew I could never return to live amongst the yetis. I was a false god who had brought them and could bring them nothing but sadness. I hadn't the heart even to look back at them as we left, but hid my face in Red's neck.

We travelled uphill through the forest, many of

the younger yetis swinging high above us through the trees, so high that they often vanished into the mist that hung about the treetops. Wherever the undergrowth became impenetrable, as it often did, Red would climb up into the lower branches, and with me clinging around his neck we would swing together through the trees with such easy power and surefootedness that I could not feel alarmed. We stopped only to drink in the streams and to glean berries from the bushes and to sleep at night. The yetis made beds of branches and twigs high up in the trees and we would climb up at dusk and lie there curled together for warmth.

For many days we journeyed upwards, ever upwards; and as time passed and the forest thinned, the yetis spoke less and less amongst themselves. They were growing increasingly wary and nervous as they left their own territory behind them. And then quite suddenly one morning we were in the bright light of the sun with the great white peaks towering around us. I had all but forgotten the mountains. The dense cloud forest I had lived in for so long seemed not to belong to this barren place of rocks and snow where scarcely anything grew or lived. When I looked below me back towards the forest we had come from I could see only clouds, a thick layer of boiling white clouds that straddled the invisible valleys all around. It was as if the forest did not exist. The yetis spread out now across the snow, bounding on downwards at a terrifying pace, pausing often to listen and look. I remembered the last time I had ridden on Red like this, on the way down from the dopkas' camp – it seemed a long, long time ago.

White Beard and One Ear led the way all that day until, as the sun went down, we stopped on the edge of a stand of fir trees and looked down into a fertile valley with a ribbon of green fields lining either side of a golden river. White Beard pointed, but we had seen them already, a flock of wandering sheep floating in unison across the slopes on the far side of the river.

Perched on a hill, its great dark walls growing from the rock, stood a gaunt monastery. Its windows caught the last gold of the sun and held it for a brief moment before they turned as black as the walls around them. Prayer flags fluttered above the walls and I could hear the sound of bells and beating drums. The murmur of distant voices drew my eyes to the river again. Two dark, bent figures carrying pails were making their way slowly up the hill towards the gates of the monastery. I should have been glad at the sound. They were after all the first human voices I had heard for over a year, but I was not. The sight of them and the sound of them filled me with dread, and the effect on the yetis was similar. They shrank silently back into the safety of the trees and crouched down to watch. There was a tension amongst them I had never witnessed before. They were frightened, but whether by the drums or the voices I could not tell.

With a deep sense of impending but inevitable

sadness I decided that it would have to be here that I must part from the yetis. Until then I had not searched for an opportunity to escape. I just felt that one day the time and the place would be right, and now I knew the time had come. Yet as Little Red put his arm around me in the gathering gloom I had no wish to leave them. I had no home to go to, no other friends. The only family I had on this earth were these innocent, loving giants who worshipped me and whom I had so deceived. Little Red stroked my cheek and fondled the lobe of my ear. My heart cried out to stay with them, and as the first glimmer of a bright moon lit the white hillside below us I weakened. Why should I go? I had lived with my guilty secret so long, why not a little while longer?

I had still not finally resolved the question as we stole out of the trees and down the hillside later that night. We made hardly a sound. We left the snow and the scree behind us as we reached the bottom of the valley and crawled on our bellies down across the open fields towards the river. No man could have leapt that river but the yetis sprang across without even having to run at it. I clung to Red and rolled off him as we landed on the other side. The sheep below the monastery had seen us or sensed us. They rushed together for protection and huddled against the walls of the monastery. From inside came the sound of prayer bells and chanting and the smell of cooking meat. The familiar scent of yak dung was heavy on the air. I heard a cough and the spit that followed.

The yetis closed in, slowly herding the sheep into a tight flock. For a few moments they crouched down on all fours and then in a flash they were in amongst them. Most were successful at the first strike. I saw Uncle, White Beard and One Ear making off towards the river, sheep slung over their backs. With the flock scattering, the others hunted down their quarry, running alongside the sheep matching their every swerve and dodge, measuring the pace, waiting for the right moment to reach out and catch a back leg. I saw Little Red leaping the river, a sheep struggling on his back. He scampered off up the hillside. Red was the last to catch his sheep and then we were running back down towards the river together. High up on the hillside I saw the yetis racing across the snow and into the trees beyond. White Beard was slower than the others and he stopped to look back at us before lumbering on through the snow. Red and I were the only ones still to cross the river. Behind us as we ran the sheep set up a chorus of bleating; and then the dogs began to bark. Torches appeared at the gates of the monastery. Red was waiting for me at the water's edge, the sheep over one shoulder. He was calling to me to hurry and held out his free arm to help me across. From the monastery came the sound of running feet and shouting. I hesitated.

We stood in the moonlight looking at each other, and he knew then I was not coming back with him. "Leelee!" he cried. "Leelee!" I so nearly went with him, but the blast of a gunshot in the night behind me cleared my thinking. I turned away from him and ran up towards the monastery. "Don't shoot," I screamed. "Don't shoot! Don't shoot!" I looked back. Red was across the river and galloping on all fours across the snow. I saw Little Red waiting for him. His father took his arm but Little Red broke free and began to run back down towards the river dropping his sheep. Red went after him and caught him before he reached the water's edge. They stood there looking at me for some moments and then they bounded up towards the trees. I watched as they became moving shadows and then part of the forest.

A few moments later a terrible cry echoed down the valley. "Leelee! Leelee!" A snarling dog tore at the sleeve of my coat and another set about my ankle. Then there were dark figures in cloaks running down towards me and rough hands pulling away the hood of my coat. I was surrounded by a rabble of angry men, shepherds I presumed them to be, for some of them immediately set about rounding up the remaining sheep. They were brandishing weapons and shouting at me in a language I could not understand. A rifle was pressing into my chest. I had lived for so long without the sound of anger that it was harsh and cruel to my ear. The dogs were pulled off me and I was led away up the hillside towards the monastery. All the while my captors shouted at me, pointing at my face and pulling my hair. I was half-carried, half-dragged in through the gates of the monastery, like some wild beast they had caught which they feared might still break free and attack them.

In the light of the courtyard I could make out shadowy figures of monks coming towards me, their robes whipped about them by the wind. Thankfully their hands were gentle, and their voices, although shrill with excitement, were kind. In the flickering, golden light under the cracking prayer flags they examined me, looking into my eyes and lifting my chin. There was much argumentation amongst them until one of them licked his finger and rubbed away the dirt on my forehead. This seemed to resolve suddenly all discussion. I was indeed a foreigner as they clearly suspected. I expected the worst, though to be honest I was so miserable by now that I no longer cared what became of me.

To my complete astonishment though the discovery of my white skin did not condemn me after all. I think perhaps the shepherds still had every intention of cutting my throat but the monks must have argued my case well, for at last I was taken into their custody and the shepherds walked away still debating and muttering angrily.

As we turned to climb the steps of the monastery I caught the faintest echo from the mountains around. "Leelee! Leelee! Leelee! Lee. . . !" Everyone stopped and listened. One or two of the shepherds clutched each other in fear. Again it came, stronger than the first time, and tugging at me. I felt a terrible urge to break free and run, but the gates of the monastery were closing fast behind the shepherds and I knew that even if I could escape, their dogs would drag me down. Besides, the hand on my elbow was gently insistent and the monks around me were welcoming. The echo died as the moon slid behind a cloud and the mountains fell silent again.

10

The buttered tea the monks offered me was too salty to be pleasant, but it warmed and filled me, and to their delight I held my bowl out for more. As I drank, they watched me intently, whispering to each other. They seemed almost frightened to talk to me. That they were talking about me I had little doubt. I felt they were deliberating as to what they should do with me. They ventured no questions. I was surprised and glad of that for I was too tired to invent a plausible story that would explain my arrival from nowhere. I put their lack of curiosity down to language difficulties or politeness. After I had finished my tea I was led away to a mattress, where I was watched over like a baby until I fell asleep.

They roused me the next morning and fed me well before taking me to the courtyard to a waiting yak. Still half asleep I found myself mounted up and with several monks as my escort I was led out through the gates. Time and again I asked them where they were taking me. I tried in English, Chinese and Tibetan, but it soon became clear they could not, or would not, understand a word I said. I tried sign language – at which I had become expert – but this just made them laugh. I gave up.

I felt under no threat from my smiling companions. Any anxiety I might have had for my own predicament was overwhelmed by a deep sadness. Every moment now was taking me further away from the yetis. I looked back across the river at the woods where we had hidden the day before and up to the snow and mountains beyond. Were they still there I wondered? Were they waiting for me, hoping I would go to them? I turned away as the tears filled my eyes and blinded me.

During the day we passed through many farmsteads and villages and at every one I was shown off with evident pride, like a hunting trophy I thought. An excited gaggle of children and dogs would pursue us through each village. The yak rocked gently beneath me, lulling me often into a half-sleep so that I was aware only of the need to balance. Bells woke me from just such a doze that evening and I saw below us a small town and a monastery standing gold and red on the hills beyond, white prayer flags fluttering. The monks called out excitedly to everyone who came running out to greet us, and a great cavalcade of children and dogs and sheep accompanied us through the town and up to the monastery gates, the children running ahead to herald our arrival.

My reception at the monastery reminded me

somewhat of my arrival among the yetis – and I found the reason for it just as impossible to understand. It seemed I was not just peculiar or different – they seemed genuinely delighted to see me. Once inside the courtyard yellow robed monks seemed to appear from all sides. I was helped down off the yak and surrounded by my escort. They brought me into the great hall of the monastery that was lit all about with hundreds of butter lamps. A dark cloth had been stretched across the ceiling and there were brocade wall hangings everywhere. It was like a vast tent. At the far end sat an old man who stood up assisted by a monk at his side. He leant heavily on a crutch under his left arm. He was helped slowly down the steps towards me. Many of the monks left my side and ran up to him, pointing back at me and laughing as they spoke. The old man listened intently, his eyes never leaving me. The great hall fell silent as he approached me. I sensed I was somehow on trial and that this was the judge who was to deliver sentence on me. I had to say something, I felt, in my defence, something to explain myself.

"My name is Ashley Anderson," I said. "I have come from China."

"I know," said the old man, and then I saw his smile and I knew who it was. "Don't you know your Uncle Sung?" he said, and he examined my face with his hands like a blind man. "It is you! It is!" he cried. We clung together and then the babbling questions flowed through our tears of relief and joy.

I suppose if Uncle Sung had been there on his own I might well have told him the whole story there and then, but overjoyed as I was to find him alive and to be with him again I felt at that moment that even Uncle Sung was a stranger to me. There were excited, unfamiliar voices all around me. Grinning, faces peered at me, and pointing hands stabbed at me. I recoiled from them all. Although I knew well enough I was safe now that I was with Uncle Sung, I still felt like a prisoner in an enemy camp. And I remembered too Uncle Sung's story of the yeti skin he had seen on a monastery wall. Any hint of where I had been and with whom might well have sent these men into the mountains to hunt them down.

I felt also that to speak to anyone of my life with the yetis would be breaking a confidence. After all, they had been my friends, my protectors and my family. No one could ever know them as I had known them. Even to try to explain how they lived or describe them would I thought be demeaning. I would keep them to myself. So the story I told Uncle Sung and the assembled monks in the great hall of the monastery was a deal more credible than the truth, as indeed it had to be.

When Uncle Sung did not return to the 'dopkas'' camp after two days I began to despair, I told them. I believed him to be dead of the cold or killed by the wolves. I knew my only chance of survival was to leave the hut to find food whilst I still had the strength. I had seen no sign of wolves for some time and ventured out into all the other sheds and shelters. It was in one of these sheds that I discovered a pile of turnips covered in sacks. Some of them were rotten but I found enough to live on for a few days. With my strength sufficiently recovered I made my way down the mountainside and at last came to a village where I was taken in and cared for so well that they would not let me leave until the spring came and the passes southwards were all clear, and even then they were reluctant to see me leave and would not let me go alone. A guide from the village led me through the high passes and would only let me go on alone once we were in sight of the monastery. That was how I came safely over the mountains.

Uncle Sung was translating for the monks sentence by sentence and that gave me time to work things out as I went along. It was thin and short on detail and I don't think I filled in the months as convincingly as I might have done, but if I read their faces right they seemed to believe it all. They watched me wide-eyed with wonder throughout. I expected and dreaded some searching questions, and indeed, as Uncle Sung explained to me, there was some earnest debate as to which village it might have been that had cared for me, but I pleaded ignorance and bluffed my way through.

They all seemed to accept it and so did Uncle Sung. He was so happy to have me back, I thought, that he must have been more concerned with the fact of my miraculous survival rather than how and when and where it had all happened. When I had finished, he simply smiled, nodded and said nothing.

Greatly relieved that my story was universally believed I was now anxious to hear what had happened to Uncle Sung. "Why didn't you come back to the hut like you said you would, Uncle Sung?" I asked.

"Oh I came back, Ashley," he said. "But I came back too late. I've told these good people how I lost you often enough. You remember I was going to bring us back some food?" I nodded. "Well, by nightfall, the day I left you, I found a village just as I thought I would, but then came the blizzard. It was a blizzard of such terrible force that no man could walk upright in it. I sheltered in the village whilst it lasted and when the wind dropped at last I set out up the mountain again to find you. By that time the snow had changed the shape of the mountain and I could not find the paths. Again and again I tried to retrace the route I had taken but I could not find my way back to you. It was a week or more perhaps before I found the 'dopkas'' camp again and when I did you were gone.

He winced as he lifted his leg and straightened it slowly and then he sat back again in his chair and went on. "I looked everywhere, Ashley. There was nothing in the hut but driven snow and ash. I searched those mountains until I knew there was no point in going on. You must remember how weak you had been when I left you. I too thought you had been taken by the wolves, or that perhaps you had gone looking for me and perished in the blizzard. I had no way of knowing, Ashley, and I could only believe the worst. Perhaps that is why I became ill – illness is as much a matter of the mind as of the body. I was too weak in the end even to leave the hut to collect fuel for the fire. I simply lay down to die. That is how I was found, near to death, by a band of traders seeking shelter in the hut. They looked after me, fed me, and when I was well enough they brought me back here on their way down south. Time and again I took search parties from the town and the monastery here up into the mountains looking for you – many of these men have come with me. So for miles around everyone knew I was looking for you, for a white boy. That was how they recognised you and brought you back to me."

"How did you hurt your leg?" I asked.

"On my way back from the mountains, the last time we went out looking for you, I slipped and fell. I broke my leg and had to be carried back. It's mending now but I thought it never would. Bones don't mend so well when you're getting old. Months I've been here now waiting for it to mend. I'd given you up, Ashley." He reached out and pushed my hair away from my face. "I was just waiting till it got better and then I was going. I can't believe it. I have to touch you to believe I'm not dreaming. Another few weeks and we'd have missed each other – we'd have thought each other dead. I was going to go back to China, back to your father. You know what made me go on looking for so long? It was the thought of facing your father and having to tell him I'd lost you." He chuckled. "If he saw you now he wouldn't even recognise you. Do you know what he'd say? He'd say, 'Get him washed, Uncle Sung'. That's what he'd say. 'Cut his hair, Uncle Sung'. You smell worse than a goat, Ashley."

"Where are we?" I asked. "Are we in India?"

Uncle Sung shook his head. "Nepal," he said. "You're quite safe here. They like everyone here – well most of them do – even foreigners with blue eyes."

I had to endure a violent scrubbing at the hands of the monks who were gleefully fascinated by my white skin. They seemed merciless in their resolve to make me whiter still, and when they had finished with me and I had had some food inside me, Uncle Sung took me away to his room to cut my hair.

It was, I recall, a tiny cell, lit dimly by a single guttering butter lamp on the table. There was a high window above us that was full of moon. A mattress covered most of the floor. I sat, wrapped in a blanket from head to foot, as Uncle Sung cut my hair, baring my neck to the cold air. "That's more like it," he said with some satisfaction when he had finished. He took me by the shoulders and turned me round to face him. He spoke softly. "One of the monks here speaks a word or two of English," he said. "So I thought I'd say nothing, not until we were alone. It might frighten them if they knew."

"Knew what?" I said.

"I wasn't quite honest with you, Ashley, I mean in the story I told you. I didn't lie to you exactly. Let us just say I didn't tell you everything. You see I did find something in the dopkas' hut when I went back for you and it's something that's always puzzled me." I was caught unprepared for what came next for I had forgotten all about it. "It was by the fire, stretched out from one side of the hut to the other, a sort of giant figure made out of ash, with stones for eyes and a stick for its mouth. It wasn't complete – much of it had been blown around the room – so I couldn't be sure, but it looked to me like a sculpture, a sculpture of some gigantic man." I could say nothing. My mind was racing but I was drained now of all invention. I was discovered. There seemed little point in lying, not any more.

"Did you do it, Ashley?" he asked. "You made it, didn't you?" I nodded, feeling his eyes on my face and not daring to meet them. I was never able to lie to him. I don't know why I thought I could. "I thought so," he went on, nodding. "That wasn't so strange, not in itself. You had to pass the time somehow, didn't you? What was stranger still was a footprint I found in the ash, twice the size of a grown man's, and with long, even toes. I'd never in my life seen anything like that. On its own it could have been an accident, a freak of the wind perhaps, but then I found two more prints just the same in the snow outside the doorway of one of the other huts. Do you know what could have made such a print?" I

113

could say nothing. "No, neither do I, but I've heard that yetis have feet just like that."

"Yetis?" I said weakly.

"I told you about them once. Don't you remember? Part man, part monkey, part god – if you believe what some people say. They're supposed to live up in these mountains. Some of these monks have even seen them – they've been known to steal sheep from the villages. You remember that lama said you had feet big enough for a yeti. You remember?"

"I remember," I said and then I found the only way out I could see. "I'm tired, Uncle Sung," I said, and I lay down on the mattress, turned my face away from him and closed my eyes.

"Of course you are," said Uncle Sung, and he pulled a coarse, heavy blanket over me up to my chin. "Happy dreams," he said, just like he used to say when he put me to bed back at the Mission when I was a little boy. Then he said no more.

Exhausted though I was I could not fall asleep that night. I stared up at the moon and could think only of Little Red and the others who would be watching the same moon from their sleeping nests in the trees. I wondered if they would get the sheep back safely to the cave, and what they would all think of me when they heard of my desertion. My mind churned with memories of them, of Uncle and Auntie chasing after the children, of White Beard's immeasurable dignity, of Shoo's fall from the cliff-face, of the word lessons around the speaking rock,

114

of fishing with Little Red, of the river and then of Tot. Always I came back to Tot and the vision of him struggling in a swirling, muddied pool crying out for me to help. It was his dreadful cry that wrenched me at last from my nightmare, "Leelee! Leelee! Leelee!"

Uncle Sung was shaking me awake, kneeling over me. "You cried out," he said. It was some time before I realised where I was and what had happened to me, that Uncle Sung was not a part of my dream. "Are you all right?" He was feeling my forehead. "You kept calling, something about 'Tot' was it? And then 'Leelee, Leelee'. Who is Leelee? Can't you tell me? Have we ever had secrets from each other before?"

"You won't tell anyone?" I cried. "No one must ever know but you. Promise me. Promise."

I no longer wanted to hold back. Until morning we sat with our backs to the wall, swathed in the blanket. I told him everything from my first confrontation with Red in the 'dopkas'' hut to the stealing of sheep from the monastery. I took the battered coronation tin from the pocket of my coat and showed him the photograph and pipe and the knife inside. At the end of it all he put his arm round me and said: "You've no need to show me the evidence. No one could make up such a story. Perhaps you have found the only Garden of Eden left on this earth. I always used to tell your father that but for the apple there would have been no temptation. It was the apple that caused the fall, not the serpent, Ashley.

115

He never agreed with me." He was holding the photograph up to the candlelight. "I wonder who he was," he went on. "They were right too, those friends of yours. You and this young priest, you're like twins the two of you, like two peas in a pod – that's what your mother used to say. But why is he dressed up like a priest? Looks almost too young to me. More like a boy. And what was he doing up in these mountains anyway?" He turned the coronation tin over in his hands, opening and shutting it. "I've seen a tin of chocolates like this – not the same picture – sent out from England to your mother it was." He examined the pipe, pulling it apart and peering into the bowl. He shook his head. "No mystery about this. And this knife is just an ordinary knife. I don't understand any of it. It's unbelievable."

"But it's true, Uncle Sung. Honest it is," I said.

"I know it is, Ashley," he said. "Sometimes the truth is the hardest to understand. All I know is you've got nothing to reproach yourself for. You weren't to know Tot would go off on his own like that." He was examining the photograph again, looking at it closely. "There's something written here. Can't read it in this light."

I read it for him. "It says 'With Mama and Papa' and then there's just two letters 'C.H.'" Reading it once again was enough to start me thinking, and I determined that night to find out who my twin was and to unravel the mystery in which I had been so inextricably entwined for so long.

We stayed in the monastery only long enough for Uncle Sung's leg to heal completely. They were happy, peaceful weeks – an oasis of comfort and calm during our arduous journey. It was a place of quiet devotion, yet not so holy as to be oppressive. Children played in the courtyard – indeed they followed me wherever I went. I can still smell the sweet incense and see the rows of copper cylinders they call prayer wheels that the monks would turn as they prayed. I can hear the bells and drums, the sonorous tuba, the whining wind that whipped the prayer flags in the courtyard into a frenzy. It was a hard place to leave but with Uncle Sung quite recovered we left the monastery behind us and travelled down south through the hospitable green valleys of Nepal.

A stranger in Nepal is always welcome, or so it seemed. More often than not we were able to ride on the back of farm carts and we never passed a village without an escort of noisy children begging us to stay, clinging to us as we passed. Even their dogs seemed less inclined to bite than they had been in Tibet. Then one afternoon as we made our way down a rutted track through the stepped fields we fell in with a group of young men – four or five of them there were. They were Sherpas, Uncle Sung told me, the mountain farmers of Nepal. They seemed intrigued by me, and Uncle Sung was repeatedly called upon to explain me to them, which he did with great patience. They laughed at me, but not in mockery. At dusk we came into a village of simple white houses built into the hillside with roofs made from juniper. As we passed by them we heard the crisp notes of a bugle cut incongruously through the air. And then I saw a Union Jack fluttering over the rooftops. The young Sherpas beside us broke into a run and we followed them down into the village. A crowd was gathered around the flagpole. Beside it stood two soldiers in strange shining black hats that sat cocked on the side of their heads. In their belts they wore short, curved knives, that I had noticed once before in the villages higher up – 'Kukris' Uncle Sung called them. Uncle Sung took my arm and we eased our way through the crowd. There were old men with medals jangling on their chests, but most were young men like those we had been walking with.

We saw them now lined up in front of a table, stiff to attention. At the table sat an officer in a green uniform with a white skin like mine and he was looking at me in utter amazement. His chair fell over as he stood up. The crowd fell silent and parted as he came over to me.

"And what the devil are you doing up here young man?"

Uncle Sung answered for me. "We've come from China," he said. "His father is still there, the Reverend Anderson of the Charlotte Anderson Mission in Ping Ting Chow. I am taking him to England, to his grandmother."

"From China?" said the officer. "You mean you came over there, over those mountains?"

"Yes," I said, delighted at the amazement in his voice.

"What, just the two of you?"

"Just the two of us," Uncle Sung said.

"S'truth!" he said. "That's a fair walk, and what's your name young man?"

"Ashley, Ashley Anderson. And this is my Uncle Sung, Zong Sung."

"Well, if you came over those mountains, you're fit enough to join my regiment."

"What?"

"The regiment, the regiment," he said, somewhat impatiently, and he could see I was still puzzled. "I'm Captain Urquhart, Captain James Urquhart, Second Ghurka Rifles. I'm here recruiting for the regiment. Come up here once a year we do. They may be little but they're the finest soldiers in the world. But by the look of you you're too young to join up just yet, but it'll be my pleasure to escort you both back to Katmandu and from there to Delhi."

And so it was that we came by lorry and by train down into India with an escort of Ghurka soldiers, into the heat and bustle of Delhi, and Captain Urquhart took us to the door of the Mission headquarters.

There was disbelief at first when we told them who we were and where we had come from and open-mouthed astonishment at our story – and that was the untrue version. "Nothing short of a miracle," said the venerable, white-haired cleric, shaking his head. "Nothing short of a miracle."

"What about my father?" I asked. "Have you heard? Do you know what's happened to him?"

There was much clearing of throats and shifting of feet and eyes before the answer came. I feared the worst, indeed I had always expected it, so when it was finally revealed that Father was alive but a prisoner of the Japanese, I laughed and jumped up and down with delight. There was obvious disapproval at my incomprehensible behaviour on receiving such news. Perhaps the yeti inside me would not let me hide my feelings. Uncle Sung laughed with me though, the tears rolling down his cheeks.

"I knew it," he said, taking me by the shoulders. "I knew it. Didn't I always say he'd be all right? Didn't I tell you?" And we danced around the Mission office like a couple of whirling dervishes, much to the horror of the sombre staff who stood around stiffly not knowing quite where to look. "So we'll go to England, like your father said. We'll go to your grandmother's," said Uncle Sung.

They seemed only too happy at the Mission to put us on a train for Bombay as quickly as possible, and there I saw the sea for the first time in my life. As I stood with Uncle Sung on the dockside staring out to sea, I remember I had the strange sensation that it was the land that moved under my feet. The sea seemed so immense that the world, I thought, must be all water with the countries and continents swaying at anchor.

120

"He couldn't have made it in seven days," I told Uncle Sung. "It's not possible."

"I used to tell your father that," said Uncle Sung. "But there again, anything's possible, Ashley. We should know that by now, shouldn't we?"

11

The SS Caledonia seemed a veritable palace of a ship. She had three majestic funnels and layers of glittering decks. Uncle Sung and I were not however destined to live in those exalted heights. We were directed to a dark, cramped cabin in the bowels of the ship where there was little air to breathe and what there was consisted for the most part of diesel fumes from the engines. We were so overwhelmed by the magnificence of the ship, by its sheer size, that this did not seem to matter much at first. Exhilarated at the prospect of the voyage ahead we stood together on deck as the ship moved away from the dock, her siren blasting, a band playing on the quayside below us. But our high spirits were to be dampened all too soon. They vanished the minute we left the shelter of the harbour behind us and began to roll on the open ocean. We were ill immediately and with the exception of a few calm days we remained ill all the way to England.

In my misery my mind went constantly back to the cave in the cloud forests, to Little Red, White

Beard, Tot and the others. They peopled my dreams and my nightmares. I passed my days and nights curled up on the bunk, clutching the coronation tin to me. Time and again I gazed into the eyes of the young priest in the photograph, and in a constant search for clues I examined every detail of the clothes and of the brick building in the background. In my desperation I even ventured upon deck and showed the photograph to one or two of my fellow passengers. They shook their heads and said it must be an old photograph, turn of the century one of them told me. Other than that they could not help me, but they did want to know how I had come by it, and why I wanted to find out who the young priest was. They were questions I could not answer, and so on Uncle Sung's advice I did not show the photograph to anyone again. Shut up in our tiny cabin we talked of little else, he and I, so that by the time we docked at Southampton I was more determined than ever to unravel the mystery that had come to obsess me.

But on landing I was at once embroiled in my new and noisy family. A total of three aunts, a dog and numerous shy cousins met us when we emerged from Customs. The cousins hid when they saw Uncle Sung. The aunts all wore hats and one of them had a fox fur wrapped around her neck. It had beady eyes that never left me. They each kissed me perfunctorily on one cheek. Uncle Sung had his hand shaken rather formally. It was a strangely cold kind of welcome. Only the dog seemed really pleased to see us. The dog was the only one whose name I could remember at first. He was called Porter, "because he carries things", said the largest of my aunts, the one who wore the dead fox. That was my Aunt Edith, I discovered later, and it was she who did all the talking.

"We've never met your father," she prattled on. "We knew of him of course from your mother, poor little Charlotte. We all miss her you know. Even after all this time we still miss her. She was the youngest of us girls and we all loved her dearly. It's quite uncanny how much he looks like her, don't you think girls?" The 'girls' in question seemed less interested in me than they were in Uncle Sung. Uncle Sung was scrutinised and I was interrogated over a sticky bun and tea in the station cafe while we waited for the train. It became clear to me that they thought Uncle Sung could not understand English for they would talk about him constantly as if he was not there. Uncle Sung did not disabuse them, but sat serenely beside me, winking at my reluctant cousins whenever they dared to emerge from behind their mothers' skirts.

"Of course Charlotte wrote and told us all about Uncle Sung," Aunt Edith went on. She leaned closer and whispered to me confidentially. "He hasn't eaten his bun. Don't they like sweet things?" She did not wait for an answer. "Charlotte said Uncle Sung taught her more about doctoring than she ever learned at the hospital in London. Difficult to believe that, isn't it? I mean he doesn't look like a doctor. But then he isn't a Christian, is he? Well, they're not, are they? I mean, they've got hundreds of gods out there haven't they – job to tell one from the other I shouldn't wonder. Still, you can't blame them can you. I mean they're only simple people. It's not their fault."

At last Uncle Sung spoke up. "There is often," he said, "much truth in simplicity."

Aunt Edith was rather more silent after that. On the train journey she hardly said a word but looked steadfastly at the fox fur on her lap as Uncle Sung told them all of the wonderful work my mother had done at the Mission, of her kindness to him, of how much she had taught him, and of our escape from China over the mountains. They listened intently, my new cousins now quite unable to take their eyes off his face.

"Well I never! Bless my soul!" Aunt Edith kept saying, punctuating the story throughout. When she shook her head I noticed the cherries on her hat began to swing frantically, and at one point I found it very difficult not to laugh. Porter sat at her feet, his nose on her lap, looking into the eyes of the fox. "Well, what do you think of that, Porter?" she said when Uncle Sung had finished. "Quite a story, isn't it?"

I felt she only half believed it and wished suddenly Uncle Sung had told her everything, yetis, wolves and all. "I wonder what your grandmother will say, Ashley. She couldn't come to meet you – she'd have liked to – but she isn't too good on her legs these days. We'll be getting off at the next station, not far to go now."

My grandmother met us at the door of the terraced house in Iddesleigh Road in Exeter, that was to become home for Uncle Sung and myself. She was frail and leant heavily on a stick, but she cast it aside as she embraced both of us warmly on the doorstep. I did not know what to say and neither did she, so we simply smiled at each other and said nothing. To Uncle Sung she said, "Charlotte wrote and told me much about you, Uncle Sung. You have a home in my house for as long as you wish it."

My first English tea of sandwiches, muffins and fruit cake was an awkward affair of clinking cups and teaspoons. My grandmother kept patting my hand and offering me more food. The skin on her hand was silk thin over her twisted knuckles. The aunts and cousins left soon after tea, and we were left alone with Grandmother. As the front door shut she laughed gaily and sank down in her chair by the fire and put her foot up. She looked at me and smiled. "I was blessed with four daughters, Ashley. Your mother was always the cleverest of them – a lot of your grandfather in her." The smile left her and her eyes clouded over. "To be truthful I've never been the same since her passing. God had no right to take her from us, Ashley, not so young. It wasn't fair, and then I lost your grandfather soon after – broke his heart it did." Her brow furrowed into an angry frown. "It wasn't right, not right at all. Still, you're here now and here you shall stay. We shall have to think about a school for you, Ashley, won't we?"

"School?" I asked.

"Of course," said my grandmother. "You might as well start tomorrow. No time like the present. You've a lot to catch up on, I shouldn't wonder." I looked at Uncle Sung aghast. He smiled at me and shrugged his shoulders. And so began my new life in England.

At home in Iddesleigh Road with Grandma, Uncle Sung and Porter, and with the extended family of aunts and uncles and cousins always in and out I was happy enough, though it was hard to get used to there being no sky outside my window. All I could see from my bedroom was the back yard, the coalshed, the privy, and the back of more houses that blocked out all but the midday sun, and there was little enough of that.

There were few opportunities to talk to Uncle Sung alone or in secret. It was a small house and anyway he was busy looking after Grandma. There seemed little prospect now of our ever discovering the identity of my predecessor amongst the yetis. We simply did not know where or how to begin the search. More than once Uncle Sung encouraged me to tell Grandma everything, and to show her the photograph – he was sure we could trust her with our secret. But I was adamant. I would trust no one. I kept the coronation tin hidden in the bottom of my chest of drawers under the drawer liner, and each night I took it out and pondered over it. I even bought some tobacco once and lit the pipe and smoked it just to see what would happen. It made me sick, that was all.

Porter and I became inseparable. I think it was because I would walk him every day down to the river and talk to him. He loved to be talked to – it made him feel important. Much to Grandma's disgust he would often come to sleep on my bed at night. She was a stickler for cleanliness – my ears and fingernails were checked each night before bed, and I could not escape baths no matter how hard I tried, much to Uncle Sung's amusement.

School was a torture to me. The formalities and regimentation I found there were alien to me. There was a severity and a stiffness about the teachers that I feared, and the early inquisitiveness of my fellow pupils soon turned to naked aggression as my shortcomings were revealed one by one. I knew no French, no Latin, even my English I spoke and spelt differently from them. They soon found out that I had no father or mother, only Uncle Sung, and I will not repeat what they said of him whenever he walked with me to school.

It was Uncle Sung's Christmas present to me that marked me out for ever as an outcast at school. He had made me another quilted Tibetan coat – my old one was in tatters. I remember it was snowing heavily the morning I put it on to go into school. In the cloakroom I was surrounded by a mob of mocking, taunting faces. "Coat of many colours", they called it. "Know what happened to Joseph, don't you?" And they began to pull it off me, tearing the sleeve. Fortunately the bell went and no more harm was done. But worse was to come. At break I was called before the headmaster who told me the coat would have to be confiscated – it was not school uniform, he said. He sent me to fetch it. When I reached the cloakroom it was deserted. I found what was left of my coat strewn around the floor in pieces. I could not keep back the tears of anger and hurt that came to my eyes. I knew then I could never be one of them.

After that I sought out no friends and none came to me. In the classroom I succeeded at nothing, but I excelled on the sports field. I found I could run faster and jump further and higher than anyone else in the school. (I put this down to my time amongst the yetis.) But far from attracting the admiration of my fellows, this only served to inflame their resentment of me, so I ran slower to divert their hostility. But the damage had already been done, and it was too late for any reconciliation.

The outbreak of war in September 1939 was a new excitement and one that I welcomed, for the new boy of uncertain origins – 'Joseph' they called me now – was forgotten. At last they left me alone. Even so I was always glad to be sick and off school, and I was frequently – the change of climate Grandma thought. But she was wrong. I was even relieved when the doctor diagnosed glandular fever and said I would have to stay at home in bed for a few weeks. The fever worsened and Uncle Sung moved his bed into my room and was beside me day and night. I would not now be parted from the coronation tin, although Uncle Sung took care to hide it away from prying eyes of visitors. Whether the coronation tin was the talisman that cured me or whether it was the doctor I do not know, but the fever left me at last.

During my convalescence I was lavished with affection. Delegations of adoring relatives would visit me each day. Grandma kept me supplied with piles of books from the library and I became an avid reader of Robert Louis Stevenson, Walter Scott and Rider Haggard. Both she and Uncle Sung would take turns to read to me when I was weak (it was a peculiar illness that left me feeling alternately quite recovered and then suddenly unwell again). But I was happier then than I had been since my time amongst the yetis. Porter scarcely left the end of my bed – more attentive than any nurse, Grandma said. I didn't really want to get better, but I did. The doctor came less and less frequently and then I was allowed out of bed so long as I stayed in my room and kept warm. He would come once more, he said, for the last check up.

The doctor was old and very deaf so he shouted when he spoke and was inclined to repeat himself. I suspected he must have believed that everyone was as deaf as he was. I liked him because he was interested in Porter. He spent as much time in petting Porter as he did examining me. "Fine dog," he would say. "I said he's a fine dog, this one. What's he called? I said what's he called?" And I'd tell him for the umpteenth time. "Water? Water? Funny name for a dog. I said it's a funny name for a dog."

I honestly do not know why I had the coronation tin out that last time the doctor came – Uncle Sung had warned me often enough to keep it hidden under my pillow during the daytime. Whatever the reasons I never heard the knock on the front door downstairs. I never heard him coming up the stairs. I was sitting cross-legged on the edge of the bed considering the photo and thinking the young priest had strangely large hands for his size, when I heard him on the landing outside the door. "You needn't come up, Mrs Carpenter," he said. "I can find my own way up by now." I just had time to climb into bed and stuff the coronation tin under my pillow before he came in.

I was sitting forward holding up my pyjama top so he could tap my back when the tin somehow slipped out from behind me and crashed to the floor. The photograph came to rest at his feet. It landed upside down. He finished listening to me and then crouched down. He put the knife and the pipe back in the tin and handed it to me. "Smoking a pipe at your age?" he laughed, and he bent again to pick up the photograph. He scarcely gave it a glance before putting it down on top of my library books. He packed away his stethoscope and clicked his bag shut. "You'll be fine enough now, Ashley," he said and he turned to go. "Back to school next week."

He had opened the door and was almost gone before he stopped suddenly and turned round. He walked back to the bedside table and picked up the photograph. "I thought so," he said. "A 'Housey' boy." And then he looked more closely. "Good gracious! Where did you get this?" It was at that moment that Grandma came in with Uncle Sung. The doctor was shaking his head. "Incredible, incredible. I'm almost sure I was at school with him, same house we were. Yes, it is him. It is. You never forget your school friends, and certainly not this one." Grandma was beside the bed now and the doctor handed her the photograph. "You know who he is Mrs Carpenter, that's 'Big Ed', Edward Lely or Sir Edward Lely as he is now. Nobel Prize winner, medicine."

Sir Edward Lely! "Leelee! Leelee!" I could hear again the last plaintive cry of the yetis.

"That must be his father and mother I suppose. Don't remember them of course. But the boy . . . looks about your grandson's age, Mrs Carpenter, bit older perhaps – come to think of it he's not at all unlike him, not at all. Remarkable. I said, he's not at all unlike your grandson, Mrs Carpenter. Well I never. 'Big Ed'. We called him 'Big Ed' on account of his brains and his size, y'know. It's him, I swear it is. Not a face you'd forget."

"What's he dressed up like that for?" asked Grandma. "Some kind of seminary is it?"

"Certainly not. My school uniform that was – blue-coat, yellow stockings, bands. 'Housey'. Christ's Hospital. 'C.H.' we always called it." I remembered then the initials on the photograph. "We were there together. Went to Medical School together, St Thomas's, up in London. Went our separate ways after that. Lost touch. I became a humble G.P. and he, well, he was always brilliant. Went into research. Circulatory discorders. Brilliant he was. Retired now, lost his mind for a bit I heard – too clever for his own good perhaps. But he's one of the greatest medical men of our generation – no doubt about that. Yes, and come to think about it he lives down here in the West Country somewhere, Honiton way I think. Haven't seen him for over forty years or more, but that's him. I'd stake my life on it."

Grandma glanced up suddenly and caught the look of panic and helplessness in my eyes. She frowned. The doctor went on. "You know him do you?" he said. "You know him?" I shook my head. "Then where did you get the photograph? I said, where did you get the photograph?"

"Found it," I said feebly, and then, "in a library book." I was pleased with that touch of desperate inspiration.

"Probably used it as a book marker I shouldn't wonder. Well you'd best send it back to him. Somewhere around Honiton he lives – shouldn't be difficult to find. If you put a little note with it, remember me to him, will you? Incredible. Quite incredible." And he was gone out of the door chuckling and shaking his head. "See myself out," he called. And we heard the front door close.

I dared not look up for I could feel Grandma's eyes on me. "Which book?" she said at last, and I could not answer.

"I think your grandmother should know," Uncle Sung said, coming round the bed and sitting down beside me.

"She won't believe me," I said.

"Why don't you try me?" said Grandma, arranging my pillows behind me. "I'm a good listener." And so she proved.

Porter slept soundly through my story but then I had already told him all about Red, Little Red, Shoo, White Beard and Tot and the others many times. At the end of it he woke up with a jolt as Grandma stood up. "Well, there's only one thing for it," she said. "We must go and see him, mustn't we? It's his photograph isn't it, his pipe, his knife, his tin? Besides, there's still a few things I don't quite understand."

The next morning, after a sleepless night, I climbed into Aunt Edith's little black car with Grandma and Uncle Sung, and we set off for Honiton, Aunt Edith talking all the way. Of the rest of us only Grandma talked, and then only to give directions. She had quite easily found out where the old man lived. He wasn't in the telephone directory, but a friend of hers who worked on the local paper – The Western Morning News it was – had made some discreet enquiries. I suppose I should have been excited at the prospect of meeting the real 'Leelee' at long last. I'd wondered about the young man in the photograph for so long; but I was filled rather with a terrible dread in the pit of my stomach as the car turned through the white gates and rattled down the drive, Aunt Edith's grisly fox fur swinging hypnotically in front of me. The car came to a halt beside a stone porch where bracken and grass grew out of the stonework. "Stay in the car Edith," said Grandma, and when Aunt Edith objected she snapped at her with her eyes and Aunt Edith said no more.

Grandma rang the bell and Uncle Sung and I waited behind her in the porch. I remember Uncle Sung put his arm around me and patted my shoulder. He always knew how I felt. There were sharp footsteps and then the door handle turned and the door opened. "Yes?" The old lady whose face peered out at us spoke in a reedy voice, her eyes staring at us in alarm.

"Sir Edward Lely's house?" Grandma said.

"He's not well," came the reply. "He doesn't see anyone." And the door began to close.

Grandma pushed her cane against the door. "I think you'll find he'll see us," she said; and ignoring the protestations she walked into the darkness of the hallway, supported by Uncle Sung. I followed, clutching the coronation tin. The place smelt of pipe smoke and floor polish. Grandma took the coronation tin out of my hand and gave it to the old lady. "I believe this belongs to him. Say we are returning it and wish to speak to him. Tell him we will wait."

12

We stood waiting in the hallway with a grandfather clock ticking beside us. I recall that each tick seemed to be a huge effort. We could hear urgent muted voices beyond a door off the hallway and then at last it opened. "My brother will see you now," she said. "But I must ask you not to stay too long. He tires easily, you know."

Coming across the carpeted room towards us was a silver-haired man in a wheelchair, a tartan blanket tucked around his legs. The coronation tin was on his lap. His cheeks and nose were laced with minute purple veins. He looked up at us out of drooping, red-rimmed eyes that were full of consternation. His hands I noticed were shaking. "Which of you found it?" he asked. Uncle Sung pressed me forward and the old man took my hand and looked anxiously into my eyes. "You've been there?" I nodded. "You saw them? You know them?"

"Yes," I said.

He turned to his sister. "You see Molly? What did I tell you? Thought I'd lost my mind didn't you? I told you about the coronation tin, didn't I? Look, here's the pipe. And here's the knife I told you about. And that's the picture of Mama and Papa they honoured like an icon. Didn't I tell you?" Tears were streaming down his cheeks. He was clutching my hand so hard that it hurt. "It did happen Molly. It did, just like I told you, and this young man is testimony to it." He looked up at Grandma and Uncle Sung. "You know about them then? You've seen them too?"

Grandma shook her head. "Ashley was on his own," she said. "They took him in and he lived with them. I know it's difficult to believe, but it's true."

"Oh, I believe it, I believe it," said the old man and he smiled at me. "We're brothers you and I," he said, taking a handkerchief from the breast pocket of his jacket and wiping the tears from his face. "I'm afraid I'm forgetting myself." He held out his hand to Grandma. "I cannot get up dear lady. These old legs have given up on me long ago. I am Edward Lely and this is my sister Molly."

"Mrs Carpenter," said Grandma. "I am Ashley's grandmother, and this is Uncle Sung who brought the boy back home safely from China."

He took Uncle Sung's hand. "But you are from Tibet, are you not?" he said. Uncle Sung smiled and bowed his head as he shook the old man's hand. "I can wait no longer," he said. "Come and sit down and tell me everything. I must know everything. Molly, come and sit by Mrs Carpenter here, I want you to listen to every word."

137

Throughout my story there were exclamations of delight, peals of laughter and frequent sympathetic interruptions. "Yes, yes, it's true. Go on. Go on," he'd say, and then again. "He does look like me. He does. You can see how they made the mistake, can't you?" At one point he took the pipe from the coronation tin, stuffed tobacco into it and then lit up, smiling broadly through the billowing smoke. I left nothing out, not even the drowning of Tot. When I had finished he took the pipe from his mouth. "Best pipe I ever had, this," he said, and he put it down in the ashtray beside him. "Mrs Carpenter, you have a remarkable grandson. And in you, Sir," he said, turning to Uncle Sung, "he has an incomparable friend, a mentor of rare courage and tenacity. As you will hear, my story is not unlike your own – I was older that's all – I was with them longer, perhaps nearly three years by my reckoning. Molly, be a dear and fetch the sketches will you. I have them in the locked drawer in my desk."

"I know Teddy," the old lady said. "It was me that made you lock them up if you remember."

"She never wanted anyone else to find out, you know," he said. "She made me promise to tell no one. Wouldn't even let me talk about it, would you? You didn't want my career ruined did you, Molly dear? And you were right I suppose. There would never have been a Nobel Prize for a man – and a man of science at that – who came back from the dead and said he's been living with yetis. I had no proof, no evidence you see, nothing." His sister brought back a folder from the desk and laid it on the table beside him. "You believe me now, Molly?" he said, reaching for her arm.

"I always did, Teddy. I always did. But I feared no one else would. They'd have dismissed you as fanciful, mad even. I had to protect you, I had to try. It was for your own sake, for your work, Teddy. You understand."

"I know dear, I know. But after all the work and all the honours I find at the end of my life that nothing has been more precious to me than my three years with the yetis. If you had met them you'd understand as he does." He smiled at me. "Do you eat muffins?"

"He does," said Grandma. "Lots of them."

"Good, then we'll have muffins and tea, Molly," he said, rubbing his hands.

Edward Lely told us his story over muffins and tea with many of the sketches spread out on the carpet in front of us, others were in a pile on his lap. As he talked he leafed through them to illustrate his story. He began with the photograph. "Christ's Hospital, C.H. that was. My old school you know. Must have been Speech Day. What do you think Molly, about 1902 was it? And that's Mama and Papa. He died soon after. It's the only photograph I had of all three of us together. I kept it with me, took it everywhere. I did a lot of climbing as a youngster – Lake District, Swiss Alps; and when they asked me to go as the doctor to a climbing expedition to the Himalayas it was too good a chance to miss. Always a keen

naturalist I was, plants, animals – like to draw them.'
He pointed at the drawings. "The Himalayan bear –
did you ever see one?" I shook my head. "Not many
of them about, but I found them. Wolves, I saw
plenty of those, but I never saw what I was really
after, a snow leopard. So I left base camp and went
off on my own looking for them. For some reason
you know, they don't attack people – can't think
why. We make enough fur coats out of them, don't
we?" At my feet I saw several sketches of snow
leopards all drawn with great life and power.

"I never saw any snow leopards," I said.

He smiled. "Not surprised. Difficult to find they
were – they live higher than any other creature – or
so I thought. In my search for them I think I went to
places no man had ever been, and then one day I
went too far and found myself in a forest, a cloud
forest so thick that light only penetrates in the
clearings, and there were few enough of those. I
wandered in circles for days, but I found my snow
leopards and I drew them. I did not go hungry for
the place abounded with berries and nuts and there
were always streams to drink from. That was where
I first saw the yetis. I was drinking one day when
they came upon me. I had heard of yetis, of course,
but being a man of science I only ever believed in the
evidence of scientific proof. None existed, so the yeti
did not really exist – that was my thinking. But even
I had to believe the evidence of my own eyes. They
were frightened at first, as indeed I was, but they came
closer and closer each day, and when I talked to them

140

they seemed to listen. They came to watch me every day by the stream and in time I followed them home."

"To the cave?" I said.

He nodded and went on. "At first I did not go inside for they appeared to want to keep me at a distance and I was quite content just to be close to them. They began to bring me food, sheepmilk and roots and berries. In the end it was one of the younger yetis who came out one evening, took me by the hand and brought me to their fireside. I became one of them just as you did. I have never known such comradeship as I experienced with those creatures." He turned to Uncle Sung and my grandmother. "It is so difficult to explain to one who has not met them, but it seems to me that in their simplicity and honesty they reach heights of nobility that we can only aspire to, and without any learning or any god, too. I made a few sketches of them and I wrote down my observations. The sketches I still have." He rifled amongst the sheets in his folder and looked up at me again without finding anything. "I was there for about three years and noted many things about the yeti. They live I believe four, perhaps five times as long as we do and therefore of course they age very slowly. They suckle their young for two years at least I discovered; and by my calculation, and it cannot be accurate of course, pregnancy lasts about fourteen months. They hunt only what they need to kill in order to survive, and as you so rightly said, young man, everything is held in common. Violent disputes are rare and quickly over.

Yetis are of a most forgiving nature. They are physically twice our size and as strong as an ox, and on four legs can run faster than any cheetah. In short, if there is a master race – and it was we who invented the term – it is certainly not ourselves. I have often thought since, that we people are the mutant line, that the yeti is in fact the true homo sapiens. Ah, here they are." And he handed me a sheaf of sketches.

There were drawings of yetis at play, hunting wolves, herding sheep, squatting around the speaking rock, swinging through the trees. There were studies of heads and hands, eyes and ears. Some of the yetis I did not know, but many were quite recognisable. There were portraits of White Beard, looking less wizened but clearly him all the same. Then there was Red who looked just like the Little Red I had known so well and several of One Ear – more of One Ear than any of the others.

"I know him," I cried. "I know him. That's One Ear, isn't it?"

"You called him 'One Ear'," said Edward Lely, and he looked delighted. "I called him 'Bozo'. I loved him like a brother." He became suddenly serious. "Indeed, my love for him was the cause of my downfall. I could not help myself – just as you could not. Bozo was caught alone out in the forest one day and attacked by a pack of wolves. When they brought him back he was badly bitten and mauled. They thought he would die. I thought he would die. What could I do? I was a doctor after all, so I patched him up as best I could, not thinking of the consequences. I had a bandage and some iodine in my medical tin – that was what it was you see, the chocolate tin, the coronation tin as you call it. I did not expect him to survive, but he did. From the moment he sat up I became a sort of saviour, a god figure who kept his magic inside his tin. The knife I had used as a scalpel and the pipe I had chewed in my anxiety were from then on perceived as the tools of my power. I thought perhaps that the adoration would wear off in time but it didn't. With every twisted limb or bruised head they would come to me for my magic and I dispensed it only too willingly – healing magic or learning magic. Every night, sitting on the speaking rock on my stool throne. I taught them to speak as I spoke. And you are right. They do indeed have extraordinary powers of recall."

"You made the stool?" I asked.

"And my bed," he went on. "All with this knife – it served as scalpel, saw, plane and chisel. I kept the tin on the ledge above my bed. You remember? They would bring flowers to it every day. I was feted like a king, worshipped like a god. And was I disgusted by my new elevation to the deity? No, not a bit of it. I enjoyed it, revelled in it. But worse – I knew that I was beginning to believe in it myself."

"Is that why you left them then?" I asked.

He shook his head and smiled ruefully. "I'm not that noble, young man. I left them because I knew one day my luck would run out and I would be found out for the fraud I was. But perhaps like you, it was also because I saw I was changing them. They

143

were not my friends any more, but my serfs. Even Bozo was becoming my slave. So, early one morning I walked out. I took nothing with me in case they should know I did not intend to come back. That was why you found the chocolate tin with my old pipe inside and the knife and the picture of Mama and Papa. How they must have gazed at that photo over the years to mistake you for me as they did. You see, because the passing of time affects them so slowly, they have no reason to believe it affects us differently. For them I would always be the same age as I was. And they only had the photograph to remember by. I had become my photograph, and when they found you, you became me. We looked alike enough to them and it was enough I suppose that you are about as tall now as I was as a young man. To them we were one and the same. And perhaps they were longing for the return of their Messiah. Perhaps they always believed I would come back. Perhaps they wanted you to be me. Who knows?"

He sat back in his chair and closed his eyes. "And so I came home. I knew the forest well enough after three years hunting with them to find my way out. I fell in with some yak herders and went with them down into Katmandu."

"I'd given him up for dead," said his sister. "Everyone had, and then one evening he walks in here and calls out – 'I'm back, Molly'. He was bursting to tell the whole world, but I wouldn't let him. He wanted to write a book about it all, didn't you? They'd have crucified him. He had his work to do and I knew that was more important, so we kept it to ourselves."

"Once I am dead, you can tell who you like, young man," said Edward Lely. "You won't mind then, will you, Molly? The sketches are the only evidence we've got. You can have those too once I've gone. You'll see to it, Molly, won't you dear? Perhaps it will do mankind good to know that we are not necessarily God's chosen, or if we are, that we've a lot of ground to make up."

He tired quickly after this, dropping off more than once before jerking himself awake. We left him sleeping in his wheelchair and his sister showed us out.

That was the last I saw of him, but some years later, just after the war was over, a parcel arrived at the house in the morning post. It was addressed to me. There was a note inside from Molly Lely. Her brother had died and as promised she was sending me the coronation tin, the pipe, the knife and a few of his sketches. Inside the tin I found a note from Edward Lely himself.

"My dear Ashley,
All yours now. Do with them what you will. And if you should go back one day (I myself have often been sorely tempted) then try to tell them that we were no gods and that there is no magic, only the truth they already know. Goodbye.
Your friend and brother,
Edward Lely"

I wish I could say that Father came home after the war and that it all ended well. But Father never did come back. Like so many others, he was never heard of again.

When I left school I went to work as an apprentice in a tailor's shop in Gandy Street, but I was never happy there. The confined spaces of the workroom and the continual rumble of the traffic outside the window drove me to distraction. I longed for the clear, clean air of the mountains and for the warmth of close companionship. Try as I did, I could never become attuned to the harshness of the people around me. I stayed a stranger.

Grandma died in her armchair one winter's afternoon and after that the heart seemed to go out of Uncle Sung. He is old and frail now and it may not be long before I am alone. Yet I will not be altogether alone. I have a family of friends far away and it is to them that I shall go, for I know my only hope of peace and contentment on this earth is to live once more with them high in their cloud forests. I do not know if I shall be able to find the place again. But I know I must try.

Joyce Dunbar
Mundo and the Weather-Child £1.95

'I HATE THE GARDEN! I HATE THE HOUSE!
I WANT TO GO BACK HOME.'

Edmund feels a stranger in the rambling house he and his parents
have moved to, and by the time winter arrives, he is utterly lost.
Unable to hear, he is locked into a solitary world of silence.

But, slowly, he discovers another world in the wild garden. There he
makes friends with the Weather-Child, who climbs and rides on the
weather, swinging on all its changes.

It is the Weather-Child who frees him from isolation and leads him
back into the real world.

Paula Fox
One-Eyed Cat £1.99

Ned was unable to resist firing the gun just once. He aimed at a shadow, a grey flicker in the autumn moonlight. His dread was that someone had seen him. Yet no one punished him and Ned's appalling anxiety and guilt grew. Was he responsible for blinding the cat?

This brilliantly perceptive and powerful novel, set in the States in the 1930s, is by the American novelist Paula Fox – winner of not only the Newbery and Hans Christian Andersen medals, but also the American Books Award for Children's Literature.

'Sometimes a rare book comes along that adults and children can appreciate with equal intensity . . . These exceptional books can be read at multiple levels of understanding; they extend fresh insights to grown-ups, yet remain within the grasp of the younger reader. Such a book is Paula Fox's latest novel, *One-Eyed Cat*'
CHILDREN'S BOOKS

Felix Salten
Bambi £1.99

When Bambi leaves the secret glade in which he is born, he learns the mysteries of the forest and the ways of the animals who live there. But there is one creature – strange and terrible – whom Bambi fears above all others. It is his greatest enemy – Man.

One of the most powerful and moving animal stories ever written, *Bambi* is about the life of a deer – the Young Prince of the Forest – who grows up to understand the harsh realities of life in the wild.

John Steinbeck
The Red Pony £1.95

This is the story of a boy, Jody, who above all wanted a pony. It is the story of how he got it, and how it died.

But Jody waited, hoped and prayed for another pony. He only had one more chance . . .

This poignant tale of a boy and his love for a pony is a modern children's classic

Catherine Storr
The Boy and the Swan £1.99

Winner of the 1987 Earthworm Children's Book Prize

The boy lived between the sea shore and the flat, marshy countryside. It was a simple, quiet life, with a two-mile walk to school.

But one day he finds a special secret: a hidden pool with a pair of nesting swans. He takes home an abandoned egg and is overjoyed when an ugly grey cygnet hatches out.

The cygnet grows to become his own special friend . . . until something happens that threatens to part them for ever . . .

Rose Tremain
Journey to the Volcano £1.95

'As they swam, their eyes stayed fixed on the volcano. The black cloud sat tight on its rim. Then, up through the black cloud and spurting high into the clear sky above it came a gush of flame, higher than any fountain, brighter than any firework . . .
"She's going!" cried Guido.'

Trouble had been brewing all summer, from the day George's mother left his father and snatched George from his London school. Escaping to his mother's old home on the slopes of Mount Etna, George found himself plunged into the heart of a large family he barely knew. Life on the mountain was exciting and different. But under the sunny slopes lay a seething mass of molten lava, waiting to erupt . . .

David Henry Wilson
There's a Wolf in My Pudding £1.99

**Twelve Twisted, Tortured, Grim and Gruesome,
Tall and Twisted Tales**

Drawings by Jonathan Allen

Was Red Riding Hood really such an angel? Who was disguised as a prince disguised as a frog? Why did a gangster help the tortoise beat the hare?

Get ready for laughter, lies, suspense and surprise as you learn the terrible truth behind a dozen famous tales.

Mary Wesley
Haphazard House £1.99

Haphazard House had been empty for years. A place of mystery, damaged by fire and lost in time.

Then Lisa and her family arrive, falling for its crooked ways and finding that the house more than lives up to its name.

Why does the village seem locked in the past? What is the secret of the invisible gardener, and who is the eerie figure that waves from the window of a room burnt long ago?

All Pan books are available at your local bookshop or newsagent, or can be ordered direct from the publisher. Indicate the number of copies required and fill in the form below.

Send to: **CS Department, Pan Books Ltd., P.O. Box 40, Basingstoke, Hants. RG21 2YT.**

or phone: 0256 469551 (Ansaphone), quoting title, author and Credit Card number.

Please enclose a remittance* to the value of the cover price plus: 60p for the first book plus 30p per copy for each additional book ordered to a maximum charge of £2.40 to cover postage and packing.

*Payment may be made in sterling by UK personal cheque, postal order, sterling draft or international money order, made payable to Pan Books Ltd.

Alternatively by Barclaycard/Access:

Card No.

Signature:

Applicable only in the UK and Republic of Ireland.

While every effort is made to keep prices low, it is sometimes necessary to increase prices at short notice. Pan Books reserve the right to show on covers and charge new retail prices which may differ from those advertised in the text or elsewhere.

NAME AND ADDRESS IN BLOCK LETTERS PLEASE:

....

Name ————————————————————————

Address ———————————————————————

————————————————————————————

————————————————————————————

————————————————————————————